DOCTOR WHO – MEGLOS

DOCTOR WHO – MEGLOS

Based on the BBC television serial by John
Flanagan and Andrew McCulloch by arrangement
with the British Broadcasting Corporation

TERRANCE DICKS

A TARGET BOOK
published by
the Paperback Division of
W.H. ALLEN & Co. Ltd

A Target Book
Published in 1983
By the Paperback Division of
W.H. Allen & Co. Ltd
A Howard & Wyndham Company
44 Hill Street, London W1X 8LB

First published in Great Britain by
W.H. Allen & Co. Ltd 1983

Printed in Great Britain by
Hunt Barnard Printing Ltd., Aylesbury, Bucks.

ISBN 0 426 20136 1

Contents

1

Abduction of an Earthling

People disappear.

There's nothing illegal about walking out of your old life, changing your name, getting another job in another town or another country.

Sometimes there may be a more sinister explanation. In criminal circles people have been known to drop out of sight – and never reappear. There are rumours that the concrete pilings that support some of our new motorways are hiding grisly secrets. Even in a small country like England there are wild stretches where a body can be hidden and never found.

Some disappearances have far stranger explanations – like the disappearance of George Morris.

Mr Morris was an assistant bank manager in a small country town. Tall, slim, with horn-rimmed glasses and pleasant open face, he was about as average a specimen of his kind as you could wish to find.

He was fortunate in that he lived close to his work. Most days he didn't even take the car. Twenty-minutes brisk walking across the common took him from the front door of the little

7

High Street bank, across a pleasantly wild and unspoiled common and up to the front door of the big house in a quiet country lane.

On this particular evening he telephoned his wife just before he left the bank and told her, as he told her every weekday evening, that he would be home in twenty minutes. Mrs Morris said, 'Yes, dear,' went to the drinks cabinet and poured him a glass of medium-dry sherry. Twenty minutes later she would hear his key in the lock.

Sometimes she found herself wishing George would be a little less predictable.

As it happened, George Morris's life was about to become very unpredictable indeed.

He strode briskly out of the town, across the common and followed his usual path which led through a clump of trees, down into the little hollow and then on home. It was a fine summer evening, he wasn't taking work home, so he was quite unencumbered, no rain coat, no brolly, not even a briefcase, and he marched smartly through the green countryside, a faintly incongruous figure in his dark business suit.

At the top of the little hollow he stopped in utter astonishment. There was a square metal shape, squatting there in the centre of the hollow. At close range it looked enormous, the size of a small building. It seemed to be made of heavy steel plates, scarred and pitted with rust. Morris walked cautiously up to it.

There was a clanking, grinding sound, and a door slid open in the side. A group of men came out, extraordinary men in wild, barbaric, vaguely military-looking clothes. The leader was big-bellied and bearded, with cunning little eyes in a piggy face. The man behind him was taller, with a stubble of grey beard on his chin. More men appeared, tough savage-looking types with oddly shaped weapons in their belts.

To Morris's indignation two of them darted round behind him, gripping his arms. He struggled wildly, but found he was quite helpless. 'What's going on?' he demanded indignantly. 'Is this some kind of student rag?'

No one answered.

The burly, bearded one, obviously the leader studied Morris thoughtfully, as if checking him off against some mental specification. Then he nodded.

The tall thin one took a small silver cylinder from his pocket and pressed it to Morris's neck. Immediately, Morris became quiet and still. He was more or less asleep on his feet as they led him into the space ship.

Slowly, lumberingly, the ship took off. It gathered speed, dwindling rapidly it shot up into the summer sky, then vanished completely as it entered hyperspace.

Morris remained under electronic sedation for the long voyage across the galaxy. It was when he awoke that the nightmare really began.

As it happened, the kidnapper's space craft was converging with another, even more extraordinary ship, a space/time craft in the form of a square blue box with a flashing ligh on top – a police box of a type used on Earth in the twentieth century.

It was called the TARDIS and it was the property—or at least it was currently in the possession of—a wandering renegade Time Lord known as the Doctor.

The TARDIS had many unusual features, among them that of being dimensionally transcendental, small on the outside, infinitely larger on the inside.

In the brightly lit central control room of the TARDIS, the Doctor was hard at work. At this time in his lives, he was a very tall man with wide staring eyes and a mop of curly hair. Much of the time he wore a long elegant coat, something between overcoat and smoking jacket, made of some reddish, velvety material and cut in a vaguely Edwardian style.

Just now the Doctor was in his shirt-sleeves, and wearing an apron round his waist. The coat, together with an incredibly long multi-coloured scarf and a broad-brimmed soft hat were hanging on an old-fashioned coat-stand, that looked strangely out of place in the control room.

At this particular moment, the Doctor wasn't actually controlling the TARDIS. He was leaving this to his Time Lady companion, Romana, a fair-haired, classically good-looking young woman with an impressively high forehead and an air of aristocratic hauteur. Romana had a great sense of her own dignity—which sometimes suffered in her association with the Doctor.

The task presently occupying the Doctor was the repair of K9, who had been temporarily immobilised by a rash dip in the sea. In appearance a kind of robot dog, K9, as he would be the first to tell you when in good health, was a self-powered mobile computer with defence capabilities. If anything, the little automaton had an even greater sense of dignity than Romana.

For the time being however, K9 was lying mute and immobile on a table, his circuits corroded by brine. The Doctor, who loved a good tinker, was happily working away at K9's innards with his sonic screwdriver, leaving Romana in charge of the many-sided central control console.

The Doctor worked absorbedly for some time, occasionally muttering to himself, odd, disjointed phrases like, 'Aha!' 'That's it' and 'Where did I put those electro-pliers?' In between times, he whistled an old Martian lullaby between his teeth.

For some reason Romana found all this very irritating. She moved around the console, adjusting controls and checking dials, shooting the Doctor an occasional glance of irritation.

At last the Doctor looked up. 'Nearly there, Romana. This is the delicate bit. You'd better stop the TARDIS, we don't want any nasty jolts.'

Romana studied the navigational console. 'We seem to be in the Prion Planetary System at the moment. We'd better land.'

The Doctor frowned. The Prion Planetary System sounded vaguely familiar, but he couldn't remember whether what was familiar was good or bad. 'Never mind, hovering will do.'

As always, Romana felt her way was best. 'You're sure, Doctor? There's a planet called Tigella that looks quite handy.'

The Doctor was brooding over K9's circuits.

'Tigella? Never heard of it.'

'Well, there's one called Zolfa-Thura as well. You must have heard of that, it's in all the history books.'

'They're all in someone's history books. What's so special about Zolfa-Thura?'

'A great technological civilisation. Supposed to have made incredible breakthroughs in energy-matrix technology. Destroyed itself in some mysterious internal war. A whole great civilisation blown away to sand and ashes. Now all that's left is the screens.'

'Quite. What screens?'

'Enormous metal screens, five of them set up on the surface of the planet for some long-forgotten purpose. The Screens of Zolfa-Thura.'

'Oh, *those* screens . . .' The Doctor's head popped up. 'Of course! I've been to Tigella. You did say Tigella, didn't you?'

'That's right.'

'Well, I've been there.'

Romana looked at him in exasperation. It was understandable that the erratic course of the Doctor's many lives should sometimes leave him confused about when and where he'd been. But did he really have to be quite so scatterbrained? 'You've been to Tigella? When?'

'Oh, some time ago. Terribly nice chap called Zastor showed me round. Remind me to get in touch with him some time. Tell you what, I'll do it now!'

He made for the control console, but Romana headed him off. 'Can't we just do one thing at a time? I'll set the controls to hover, Doctor, you finish repairing K9, *then* we'll send a message to Tigella.'

'First things first, eh?' said the Doctor approvingly.

'Exactly.'

'Though not necessarily in that order.' With this baffling observation, the Doctor went back to his work.

Deep below the surface of Tigella they were in trouble. It is no easy matter to move a whole civilisation underground. Without the natural resources of sun and air and running water, you need power, a great deal of it – power for heat and light and air-conditioning, power for hydroponic farms, for food storage and a hundred other needs. Fortunately, the Tigellans had power in enormous quantities, power from a unique inexhaustible source, that was the centre of their religion and basis of their civilisation, the Dodecahedron. A great crystal had mysteriously descended from the skies in the distant past. Now enshrined in the Power Room, the Dodecahedron was the mystic, glowing core of all Tigellan life.

But the Dodecahedron was failing. Not completely of course, or even continually. Some of the time it glowed as brightly as ever, powering the entire underground civilisation. But recently, the power had begun to fluctuate. Sometimes it would suddenly fail, sometimes, even more dangerously, there would be an unexplained surge. And the fluctuations were getting more frequent . . .

The whole of the interior of Tigella was

honeycombed with caves and tunnels. Over the years these had been extended and developed by the Tigellans as their civilisation grew. The Tigellans called them walkways, and here or there one might still see a patch of exposed rock behind the metal cladding of the tunnels, or the occasional rock-walled chamber, still in its natural cave-like state.

At the end of one of the service tunnels, close to the Power Room, an attractive young woman called Caris was frantically at work on a smoking control panel, watched by a terrified, white-faced technician. The panel had suddenly gone into overload and Caris had been sent to deal with it. She was a Savant, one of the scientific and technical caste of Tigella, and like the rest of her Guild she wore a neat white quilted jacket, trimmed with black at the belt and collar, black trousers and boots. Her shining yellow hair was neatly trimmed in a plain functional style.

Working against time, Caris struggled frantically to replace a burnt-out power unit and prevent a major overload. She had almost succeeded when another inexplicable power surge made all her work in vain. She looked at the power gauge and shouted, 'Look out, it's going to blow!' Covering her face with her hands Caris threw herself backwards, just as the panel exploded with a blinding flash.

The technician at her side was not so quick, or not so lucky. He fell screaming to the floor, his hands to his face.

Caris operated her portable communications set, relieved to find it still working. 'Emergency,

emergency! Burn-out on walkway nine. Medical and lighting assistance needed immediately.'

Not far away in Central Control Caris's voice came crackling out of a loudspeaker. The enormous control room, lined with instrument panels from floor to ceiling, was the nerve centre of Tigellan civilisation, monitoring and controlling the energy flow produced by the Dodecahedron in the Power Room. Now the power was out of control, and here too lights were fading and brightening again, dials flickering wildly.

At the main control desk sat Deedrix, one of the inner group of Chief Savants, monitoring the flow of emergency messages, and issuing orders to deal with the crises that constantly arose. He wore the same neat black-and-white uniform as Caris, and like her, his blonde hair was trimmed short and neatly brushed. There was a close resemblance between all the Savants – their enemies said they all looked and thought alike.

Deedrix acknowledged Caris's message and issued a rapid stream of orders. He switched back into Caris's circuit. 'Are you hurt, Caris?' There was more than professional concern in his voice. He waited tensely until Caris's voice came back.

'No. One of my technicians got a flash-burn, but it's not too serious.'

'Good. Medical detail has been despatched.'

Another message came through. 'Air Purification Unit One is malfunctioning.'

Deedrix switched to another channel. 'Open air vents three to eight in Unit One.'

A shadow fell across the control desk, and he

glanced up to see a cowled figure standing over him. Deedrix jumped to his feet. Despite the simplicity of his monk-like robe, this tall white-haired old man was perhaps the single most important person on the planet. This was Zastor, Leader of all Tigella.

'Forgive me, Zastor, I did not see you enter.'

'Be seated, Deedrix, this is no time for ceremony. You must continue with your work.'

Another message came through, though this time a reassuring one. 'Power levels steady on all fronts. Irrigation levels holding.'

Deedrix gave a sigh of relief. 'Thank you. Clearing all channels.' He slumped back in his seat. 'That seems to be it – till next time.'

Zastor looked compassionately at his weary face. 'Well, Deedrix, how bad is it?'

Deedrix said steadily, 'Very bad indeed, sir. We can't control the power levels much longer. If these surges go on there'll be complete breakdown – and the end of all Tigella.'

2

The Deons

Zastor looked worriedly at Deedrix for a moment. The young Chief Savant was one of the most brilliant members of his Guild – and one of the most cool-headed. A man to underplay a crisis, rather than exaggerate . . .

Zastor glanced round the gleaming control room with its multiplicity of multi-coloured control panels, their lights winking steadily. 'All this, and yet you are helpless? So much for science.' Even as he spoke Zastor knew the criticism was unfair.

Predictably, Deedrix sprang to the defence of his Guild. 'We can do nothing without a detailed investigation of the Dodecahedron, and that the Deons will not permit!'

'That is so,' agreed Zastor, sadly and a little helplessly.

Although Zastor was Leader of Tigella, he ruled over a divided people. Everyone on Tigella belonged to, or at least supported, one of two groups – the Savants and the Deons. Evenly matched in size, power and influence, the two groups were irrevocably opposed over one crucial factor – the Dodecahedron. To both parties the

Dodecahedron was a kind of miracle, mysterious and all powerful. Even its arrival on the planet was shrouded in mystery. Legend said simply that it had descended from the skies.

To the Savants, however, the Dodecahedron was a miracle of science, to be studied observed and ultimately used to benefit Tigellan civilisation. Most leading Savants agreed that the energy they were drawing from the Dodecahedron, sufficient though it was to power the entire planet, represented but a fraction of the device's potential.

And there was the difference. To the Savants the Dodecahedron was a device. To the Deons it was a god.

Now that the Dodecahedron seemed to be failing them, the reactions of the two parties were more opposed than ever. To the Savants the power surges were a malfunction, to be investigated and corrected. To the Deons, they were punishment for the sins of Tigella, to be dealt with by penitence, meditation and prayer.

The only link between the two factions was Zastor – a Leader with no real power to act, since he had always to balance one side against the other. At the same time Zastor was a figure of supreme importance, since he alone could save Tigella from a bitter civil war. It was not an easy position.

Zastor looked sympathetically at the angry young Savant. 'I understand, Deedrix. Believe me, I understand.'

'I've always argued–' began Deedrix.

Zastor chuckled. 'That is most certainly true!'

Deedrix gave a reluctant smile – trust Zastor to defuse the situation – but he was not to be distracted. 'For thousands of years our lives have been dominated by a mystery. The Dodecahedron belongs to all of us, not just to the Deons.'

'Whatever you think of their opinions, their religion deserves respect.'

'Religion,' snorted Deedrix. 'I might just as well worship this control console.'

'Perhaps you do in a way,' said Zastor gently.

Deedrix sighed and gave up the argument. He touched a control. 'Control to walkway nine. Update on the burn-out, please.'

In the walkway, Caris straightened up from her work, mopping her forehead. The burned technician, a dressing on his face, was being lifted onto a stretcher by the medical team. Caris and a replacement technician were working under emergency lighting from portable power packs, welding a new transformer into place.

Caris spoke into her com-unit. 'I'm replacing the transformer now, Deedrix. There'll be no power for about three hours.' Bitterly she added, 'Now will you believe I'm right?'

Deedrix said formally, 'Thank you, Caris. Acknowledged and understood.' He looked challengingly at Zastor. 'Caris seems to feel that recent events add weight to her arguments.'

'This ridiculous scheme of hers to re-inhabit the surface, face the attacks of the vegetation?' Zastor shuddered. 'It would take years of preparation.'

19

'Decades, more likely.'

'So, we agree for once?'

'As it happens I don't much favour the idea myself,' admitted Deedrix. 'There are better ways in my view – like learning to use the full power of the Dodecahedron.' He leaned forward urgently. 'But at least Caris and her friends have a plan – a rational, scientific plan.'

'A plan which the Deons have declared a blasphemy.'

'You could over-rule them, Zastor!'

'And how long would I remain Leader if I did?'

It was the old dilemma. If Zastor was seen to favour either side he would be instantly overthrown, to be replaced in all probability, by someone far worse.

'I know your problems, Zastor. But I tell you this, and I speak as a Savant, one who has worked all his life to understand these things. Unless somebody does something soon, our safe and bountiful city may well be on the edge of total extinction. You are leader, Zastor – the responsibility is yours.'

Zastor brooded for a moment, and then bowed his head. 'Very well. I will send a message to Lexa.'

In the cathedral-like hush of the huge Annexe to the Power Room, Lexa, High Priestess of the Deons, was deep in meditation, surrounded by her purple-robed acolytes. They were grouped round the great triangular rock that dominated the centre of the room.

Lexa was a tall handsome woman, sumptuously

dressed in the elaborate regalia of a Deon priestess, her long hair hanging free from beneath her high-crowned ceremonial head-dress.

It was dark and silent in the huge circular chamber, lit only by flames of the ceremonial torches in their brackets on the walls, and occasionally by the fitful glare that came from the arched doorway to the Power Room.

The acolytes, robed and head-dressed like Lexa, though less elaborately, sat around her in a semi-circle, soothed and half hypnotised by the low energy-hum that came from the Power Room. This was the Ceremony of Concurrence, the most important ritual of the Deon religion.

Lexa looked up in annoyance when the black-uniformed, black-helmeted guard appeared in the doorway of the Annexe. 'Well?'

The guard approached, bowed deferentially and handed her a scroll, bearing Zastor's seal.

She opened it, read the lengthy message and rose angrily to her feet. 'No!'

The acolytes crowded round her, but dared not speak.

'No!' said Lexa again. 'Zastor is our Leader, but he has no right to lead us into sacrilege!'

She waved the acolytes back to their places. 'Resume the Concurrence. I shall explain this matter to Zastor and the Savants – yet again!'

The acolytes bowed their heads. Lexa strode determinedly from the Annexe, and along the walkway to the stairway that led to the higher levels. As she reached the bottom of the staircase, she saw Zastor waiting at the top. It was typical of him that rather than waiting for her to attend him, as was his right as Leader, he had come to escort her.

When they reached the top of the staircase, Zastor said disarmingly. 'I see that you are angry, Lexa.'

'It is not me whom you have angered, it is the Power,' replied Lexa forbiddingly.

'For the moment at least, its anger seems to be under control. And so perhaps should ours be.'

They began walking along together. 'The Savants have some proposals,' Zastor went on. 'Proposals that will help to solve our poblems, or so they believe.'

'Belief!' scoffed Lexa. 'It is a word too great for their small minds. They are children, wilful, ignorant and lost.'

'We shall all be lost, Deons and Savants alike – if the Power fails us.'

'Where are we going?' asked Lexa.

'To the debating chamber, to listen to the proposals of the Savants,' replied Zastor placidly.

'I warn you, Zastor, this is not a matter for compromise.'

'Lexa, I'm an old man, with less faith, perhaps, than you. Yet I think you trust my judgement, do you not?'

After a moment's pause Lexa said grudgingly, 'Yes . . .'

'Then hear the proposals of the Savants. They ask only to be allowed to make a few measurements, some calculations. They will not even touch the Dodecahedron.'

'They will not even enter the Power Room,'

said Lexa grimly. 'No one can revoke our ancient laws – not even you, Zastor.'

It was unfortunate that at this precise moment they were passing the door to Central Control just as Deedrix came out on his way to the Debating Chamber, and he joined in the argument. 'And not even your precious Concurrence, Lexa, can revoke the laws of science.'

Lexa rounded angrily on him. 'Now see here, Deedrix –'

Zastor stepped between them. 'Deedrix, Lexa, enough of this squabbling. Try to act like leaders.'

'Then lead us by example, Zastor. Make a decision!' urged Deedrix.

For a moment Zastor looked tempted, then he shook his head. 'I cannot choose between one side and the other.' He sighed. 'I was afraid it would come to this. However, I have taken a decision of another kind.'

Deedrix and Lexa looked at him in astonishment.'

'Some fifty years ago,' said Zastor, 'I knew a man who solved the insoluble by the strangest means. He seemed to see the threads that bind the universe together, and have the ability to mend them when they break.'

'A Savant?' asked Deedrix sceptically. 'Or a mystic, like Lexa here and her acolytes.'

'A little of each, I think, and much more of something quite different. As it happens he is near by, and he has asked to visit us. I have invited him to do so.'

Deedrix frowned suspiciously. 'You're invited an Alien – here?'

Zastor nodded.

'Why?' demanded Lexa.

'I think this situation needs his delicacy of touch.'

At that particular moment, the Doctor's delicacy of touch was being used to make a few final adjustments to K9's circuitry. 'The reflexes seem to be all right now . . . but he'd better stay out of the sea in future, or he'll find himself in deep water.'

'It's hardly his fault if someone forgot to sea-proof him!'

'Yes, quite,' said the Doctor vaguely. 'Do you know where I put his manual?'

'Yes, Doctor.' Romana went to retrieve the manual, which was wedged under the too-short leg of the hat-stand, another of the Doctor's emergency repairs. She handed it to the Doctor.

'K9 had better be all right, we may need him on Tigella.'

'The Tigellans aren't hostile.'

'The plants are, Doctor. According to my intergalactic guide and history, the surface of Tigella is covered with lush aggressive vegetation.'

The Doctor flipped through K9's manual, 'You don't want to believe all you read in books, you know.'

'According to the history books, Doctor, it was the lush aggressive vegetation that made the Tigellans retreat beneath the surface. Didn't you notice it when you were there?'

24

'It was reasonably friendly to me, I think. Mind you, that was quite some time ago.' He looked up from the book. 'Post Repair Test Questions, it says here. Number One: Can you hear me?' He leaned towards the little automation. 'Can you hear me, K9?'

'Affirmative – Mistress.'

The Doctor sighed. 'Not the most promising start. Pass me my sonic screwdriver, would you Romana?'

In the Debating Chamber on Tigella the debate, or rather the row, was in full swing. The tiered ranks of seats were packed, Savants on one side, Deons on the other, and in a very short time the debate had degenerated into a shouting match.

Zastor was on his feet. 'Savants! Deons!' he shouted. 'Remember the dignity of this place. Have we come here to squabble? If we cannot have agreement, let us at least have order!'

He sat, and for a moment, there was a rather chastened silence.

Then Deedrix jumped up. 'I've said all I have to say. I'm just wasting my time here. I'm needed back in Main Control.'

Before he could leave, Lexa was on her feet. 'Do not let him leave. He should be arrested for heresy.'

'And crushed to death, no doubt,' sneered Deedrix.

Lexa glared furiously at him. It was unfortunately true that in the early days of the Deon religion, offenders had been punished, or sacrificed, by ceremonial crushing beneath a huge rock. There had been no sacrifices for many years now, though in view of the recent troubles, some of the more conservative Deons were in favour of reviving the custom.

'You will respect the Deon laws, Deedrix,' said Zastor sternly.

'How can one respect a creed that practices the cruel and primitive rite of human sacrifice? Is that how you propose to deal with our present troubles, Lexa, by making sacrifices to your monstrous myth?'

'Remember where you are, Deedrix,' said Zastor wearily. 'Be silent!'

'No! This should be said – and before all Tigella. The Dodecahedron is no god. It is an artefact. It was *engineered*!'

This horrifying blasphemy drew a howl of protest and rage from the Deon acolytes. Fierce and exultant, Lexa's voice rose high above them all. 'The Dodecahedron descended from the heavens. It is our god!'

'Not from the heavens,' shouted Deedrix desperately. 'From somewhere – anywhere, but not the heavens.'

Triumphantly Lexa confronted him. 'Then from where, Deedrix? *Where*?'

It was the one unanswerable question. Defeated, Deedrix turned away.

3

The Screens of Zolfa-Thura

A fiery red sun blazed out of a clear blue sky onto burning yellow sands. Barren and featureless the desert stretched away in all directions. Only one thing — or, to be strictly accurate, five things — dominated the empty landscape: the screens. Five colossal metal screens of gun-metal blue, tilted at an angle to the heavens, propped up by massive metal supporting struts: the Screens of Zolfa-Thura.

A squat ugly shape appeared out of the clear blue sky. Down and down it came, revealing itself as an ancient star-ship, a blunt square shape of pitted and rusted metal plates, a flying junkyard, an intergalactic scrapheap. It thumped clumsily down on the wide expanse of sand between the screens.

The door creaked open and General Grugger swaggered out onto the sands; Grugger the Gaztak, burly, big-bellied, in boots and breeches and a long military overcoat covered with decorations, to none of which he was in the least entitled, with an extraordinary hat on his head, a cross between a Roman helmet and a flower-pot, all jewelled and spiked. Little squinting eyes in a cruel piggy face glanced round cautiously, alert for ambush.

Behind him was Brotodac, his second-in-command, a great creaking skeleton of a man, with a stubble of white beard covering a long bony toothless chin, and wearing an assortment of military finery even more tattered than that of his chief.

Behind these two came their men, a motley, ragged, fierce-looking band. Gaztaks – the scum of the galaxy. Dressed like their chiefs, in whatever scraps of uniform they could lay their hands on, wearing an assortment of knives, swords and blasters of all shapes and sizes, murderers, mutineers, space-pirates, thieves, deserters, the criminal ragtag and bobtail of the cosmos.

There were hundreds, perhaps thousands of Gaztak bands like this. They roamed the galaxy in their battered old space-ships, living on whatever pickings they could find, looting and stealing from anyone weaker than themselves. Grugger's band was typical enough, though perhaps rather smaller than most. General Grugger had once led a little mercenary army, carried in a mini-fleet of battered space-cruisers. He had hired out to a local warlord on a primitive planet on the edge of the galaxy. Things had gone well for a while, but Grugger had made the mistake of choosing the wrong side.

After the last disastrous battle he had been lucky to escape with just one ship and a handful of men, and of course the faithful Brotodac, the one person who never lost faith in Grugger's military genius.

That was why General Grugger and his band had been reduced to accepting what was little more than an odd-job. The pay offered was good though – not that they'd seen any of it yet.

Brotodac looked disgustedly around him. 'Sand everywhere, nothing but sand. The whole planet!'

Grugger squinted thoughtfully up at the nearest of the towering screens. 'There's these things.'

' "Bring an Earthling to the Screens of Zolfa-Thura" ', quoted Brotodac scornfully. 'I never liked this job.'

Grugger beckoned to two of his men, and they led the still-dazed Morris out of the ship. He was conscious now, in a confused sort of way, conscious and terrified.

Grugger looked at him. ' "Male human, Caucasian, about two metres tall," ' he said in a satisfied voice. 'Just what the client ordered.'

'All right, we've delivered him. So who pays us?'

Strange choking sounds were coming from Morris's throat.

'Seems to be trying to say something,' said Grugger without much interest.

Brotodac was still looking suspiciously around him. 'This could be a trap, you know!' He glared at the terrified Earthling. 'Him say something? What does he know?'

'Nothing,' croaked Morris. 'I don't know anything. What have I done?'

'No one knows anything,' said Grugger morosely.

'But why me?'

'Why any of us? You don't think I do this through choice do you?'

Sobbing with fear, Morris made a feeble attempt to escape from his guards.

Grugger yawned. 'Better give him another one.'

Brotodac fished out his silver cylinder and slapped it on Morris's neck. Morris became quiet and still.

'I still think the message was genuine,' said Grugger obstinately. 'We'll wait.'

'Genuine?' growled Brotodac. 'We don't even know who sent it. There's no one here. Let's kill the Earthling and go.'

'Go where?' asked Grugger. 'Let's try thinking for a change.' He nodded towards the Earthling. 'Now why would anyone send clear across the galaxy for a creature like that?'

Brotodac thought. But the question was too difficult. He gave up. 'No idea.'

'Me neither.'

Suddenly the ground before them began to shake. The Gaztaks leapt back suspiciously, reaching for their weapons.

Some little way ahead of them, between the screens an enormous square structure was rising out of the sand. The upper section was transparent, with some kind of pillar glowing inside, the lower part gleaming and metallic. The Gaztaks stared in astonishment as what was obviously a very large building, rose before their eyes out of the sand.

Fully emerged, it was a massive gleaming

square structure, crowned with a transparent tower that looked somehow incomplete. A door slid open in the side of the building, and cool greenish light gleamed enticingly from inside. Everything was silent.

Grugger began moving towards the door.

Brotodac caught his arm. 'Don't! It must be a trap.'

'Shut up. Follow me.'

Followed, at a cautious distance, by some of their men, they headed for the open door.

On the threshold, Grugger paused for a moment, then went inside. Brotodac followed.

They found themselves in a larger room, full of mysterious equipment, humming silently to itself. There were rows and rows of gauges, dials and control consoles, some free-standing, some built into the walls. What it was all for, why it had all risen so magically out of the sand, Grugger hadn't the faintest idea.

On a stand in the centre of the room stood a huge cactus, almost the size of a man.

Brotodac prowled round suspiciously. On top of one of the consoles he found a mysterious metal instrument, L-shaped, set with controls and a tiny screen. Instinctively, he scooped it up and slid it into one of the many pockets of his tattered military coat. It was standard Gaztak procedure to steal anything that wasn't actually nailed down.

A deep slurred voice said, 'Arrival noted. Welcome, gentlemen!'

Brotodac whirled round suspiciously, fearing he had triggered some alarm.

31

'Don't be afraid,' said the voice mockingly.

Grugger was frankly terrified, but he managed to summon up a sneer. 'Afraid? Me? Who do you think you're talking to?'

'General Grugger, I presume, and Lieutenant Brotodac, together with their little band of fortune-hunters. There should also be an Earthling about somewhere.'

Grugger nodded to one of the men in the doorway. 'Bring him.' He looked around. 'And you – what are you?' Already a wild suspicion was forming in his mind.

'Forgive me,' said the voice smoothly. 'Most remiss of me. I am Meglos, only survivor of this planet.'

Brotodac stared at Grugger in total bafflement. Grugger shrugged, and nodded towards the great cactus.

'Well observed, General Grugger,' said the voice. 'I am the plant. A xerophyte to be precise.'

Morris was shoved into the room by his guards. Grugger beckoned and the Earthling was brought to a halt in front of the plant.

'Excellent, General Grugger,' said Meglos. 'You have served me well. Now, I have a real proposition for you . . .'

In the debating chamber on Tigella, the wrangling was still going on, with Zastor vainly trying to keep order. 'This chamber will yield to my authority.'

'You've lost it,' said Deedrix mockingly. 'Delegated it to the Alien friend of yours.'

For once Lexa was in agreement with him. 'A

Time Lord, a non-believer. How can we trust him?'

'The Doctor's good faith is beyond question, ' said Zastor.

Deedrix laughed bitterly. 'Faith! That word again? What we need is knowledge.'

'The Doctor brings that too.'

'We have knowledge here, if only you would allow us to use it!'

Lexa stood up. 'These arguments go round and round, and accomplish nothing. I shall seek guidance from the Power itself.'

She was about to leave when Caris burst into the room, her hands and face still smudged with the grime of her work. 'I have something to say to this chamber.'

'No,' shouted Lexa, and a howl of protest from the Deon faction came to support her.

Zastor held up his hand. 'Caris has risked her life often to help this city. Let her be heard.'

Gradually the tumult died down.

Caris faced the assembly. 'Even if we manage to restore the Power – or as the Deons would say, if the power condescends to restore itself – the bulk of the frozen food stocks will be spoiled. We shall have to return to the surface.'

The Deons, and some Savants too, shouted in protest.

When Meglos finished speaking, the two Gaztak leaders were silent for a moment, stunned by the sheer audacity of the proposition.

Then Brotodac looked at Grugger. 'He's crazy. Let's get our payment and go!'

33

'Gaztaks!' sneered Meglos. 'Pillagers of the galaxy! Thousands of little marauding bands like yours. And what's it all for?'

'Loot!' said Brotodac simply.

'The motley collection of useless trophies! How long have you been accumulating them?'

'We've done it all our lives,' said Brotodac proudly.

'And you accuse me of wasting your time.'

'Look,' said Grugger heavily. 'What you're asking us to do is impossible.'

'Not impossible – simply beyond your comprehension.'

'There's only one way into that city: through a man-eating jungle. And those Tigellans will guard that Dodecahedron with their lives; it's a god to them.'

Brotodac nodded. 'That's right. And even if we reached the thing, they say it's too dangerous to touch.'

'Really, gentlemen,' said Meglos wearily. 'Do you think I haven't considered the hazards – and found ways to deal with them? But perhaps you're right to refuse. Your timidity worries me. I see you're not interested in real wealth, real power. So if Lieutenant Brotodac will return my Re-dimensioniser, we'll conclude our business.'

'Give it back, you fool,' snarled Grugger. 'What use is it to you? What do you know about mass conversion mechanics?'

Sulkily Brotodac produced the Re-dimensioniser and slapped it back on the console.

Thoughtfully, Grugger lowered his bulk into a chair. 'Let's not be too hasty, Meglos. I'm not saying I'm not interested, but I want to know a lot more about all this before I decide.'

The Doctor stared moodily down at the prone K9. 'Bit of a nuisance if we have to reprogramme all his constants.'

'It'll take forever,' said Romana gloomily. 'I'm worried about the power depletion. At this rate, he'll need re-charging about every two hours.'

'Oh, I'll soon fix that. I happen to be an expert on power sources.'

'I see. This little job on Tigella won't take you long then?'

'Flying visit!' said the Doctor airily. 'All it needs is a quick service.'

'What exactly is the energy process, Doctor? Baryon multiplication?'

'Yes, something like that. They didn't actually let me look at it last time. Religious objections you see . . .'

'So the Dodecahedron was actually made here, on Zolfa-Thura?'

'Correct, General Grugger. Those primitive fools of Tigellans are using only a fraction of its potential.'

'A fraction? It powers their entire planet!'

'A mere fraction. These present fluctuations are simply part of its in-built programming. In its re-start mode, its output will be raised to a point where it could feed an entire galaxy.'

'That's impossible.'

'Within your limited frame of reference perhaps,' said Meglos impatiently. 'Now that terms are agreed, shall we begin? You are clear about the procedure?'

Grugger rose, went over to the main console and stood frowning down at it. He stabbed at a control. Two transparent plastic cylinders descended part-way from the ceiling, hanging suspended.

At a nod from Grugger, a couple of his men led the Earthling forward, positioning him under one of the cylinders. Then they moved the plant on its stand until it was under the second cylinder.

Grugger pressed another button and the two cylinders came down till they reached the floor, completely enclosing both Meglos and the Earthling, each in a separate container.

Meglos's voice boomed from within his transparent prison. 'Now, General Grugger, have I explained the procedure clearly?'

'Oh yes, I think I've got it clear.' Grugger pointed. 'This button starts the transference process. This one releases you when it's finished.'

'Excellent! Then let it commence.'

Grugger winked at Brotodac. 'Oh yes, we'll definitely let it commence.'

Grugger walked round the container holding Meglos. He reached out and shook it, ensuring that it was firmly secured.

Brotodac looked on uneasily. 'Shouldn't we get on with it? He looks ready to me. This button wasn't it?'

As Brotodac moved towards the controls, Grugger snapped, 'Get away from there.'

'What's the hold-up? I want to get off this planet.'

'So do I.' Grugger waved his hand around the room. 'But it would be a great pity to leave all this behind.'

Brotodac beamed, his faith in Grugger vindicated. 'You've got a plan! We're going to leave him locked in there, steal everything we can find and then clear off!'

Grugger slapped his hand down on the nearest console. 'How much do you reckon this would fetch on Pelagos?'

'Five million credits?' suggested Brotodac hopefully. 'We've struck lucky, haven't we?'

'Lucky?' Grugger tapped his own forehead significantly. 'Brains, my lad.' He looked round the room, pointing here and there. 'We can take that main console for a start. Be pretty heavy, though.'

'We could break it up.'

'And lower the value? It's a nice piece that!'

Brotodac grinned happily. Looting was something he knew and loved. 'I'll get the others.' He went to the door, tried it and turned round indignantly. 'It's shut.'

'Then open it!'

'It won't open.' Brotodac frowned. 'It opened all right when we came in – automatically.'

The voice of Meglos said. 'Exactly, gentlemen. Automatically!'

Grugger looked at Brotodac. 'He's trapped us.'

'Didn't trust us,' said Brotodac mournfully.

Meglos laughed evilly. 'Nothing so petty. I knew that as ardent pragmatists you would feel bound to attempt some variation of our arrangement, some adjustment to your own advantage. I wanted it to come sooner rather than later – so you could realise its futility.'

Grugger and Brotodac looked crestfallen.

The hateful, triumphant voice went on. 'I know you and your kind so well. If we are to co-operate, I want you to know me!'

Still Grugger and Brotodac found nothing to say.

'Well, gentlemen,' said Meglos silkily. 'Shall we now resume our original arrangements?' The voice hardened. 'Or shall we all descend into the earth together for another thousand years?'

4

Time Loop

There was an awkward silence.

Grugger cleared his throat. 'I'm prepared to forget all about this incident!'

'I do hope not, General Grugger!'

Brotodac understood the implied threat. 'We'll remember! We'll remember!'

'Good. The second button please.'

Grugger pressed the second button and both cylinders lit up. Grugger and Brotodac stood watching in fascination.

Gradually the giant cactus that was Meglos began to shrivel and deflate. It shrank and shrank until it was no more than a spiky green blob on the floor of the container.

At the same time the body of the Earthling went rigid, and slowly took on the green colour of the cactus. Little spikes appeared on the skin of the face and hands, as gradually the personality of Meglos took over the Earthling's body.

'I don't believe it,' muttered Brotodac.

Grugger pressed the third button and the green spiky figure of the Earthling stepped out – speaking with the voice of Meglos! 'We must work quickly. I've intercepted a Tigellan message.' Meglos hurried over to a communications console, adjusted controls and a diamond-shaped vision screen lit up. A face appeared on it, the face of a tall curly-haired man.

Data began to flow across the bottom of the screen.

Grugger glanced at it. . . . *usually known as the Doctor. Planet of origin: Gallifrey. Age . . .*

He could make nothing of it and turned away. 'Who is he?'

'A travelling Time Lord known as the Doctor—whose travels I shall now interrupt!'

Meglos went over to yet another console and moved between one and the other making a series of delicate adjustments. 'Now, exactly where is he?' he muttered. 'And when?'

The Doctor had taken off his apron, was pacing up and down the TARDIS control room, leaving the final fiddly bits of K9's repairing to Romana, who had changed into a kind of red-velvet trouser suit for her trip to Tigella.

The Doctor was deep in thought, and scarcely seemed to hear when Romana spoke to him. 'Where did you put the electro-pliers, Doctor?'

'In a cave . . . a sort of shrine,' said the Doctor answering a thought of his own.

'The electro-pliers?'

'No, the Dodecahedron, on Tigella.' He stared at Romana. 'What?'

'The electro-pliers?'

The Doctor fished in his pockets. 'Here.'

'Thank you.' Romana made a final adjustment, and K9's eye-screens lit up, his ears swivelled, and his tail antenna wagged. 'I think I've nearly finished.'

'Perfectly understandable they should be in awe of the thing,' said the Doctor, continuing his conversation with himself. 'Their whole way of life depends on it.'

K9's eyes went dim, and his antennae drooped. 'Oh blast!' said Romana. 'Here we go again!'

Distracted, the Doctor tripped over the now wobbly hat-stand, knocking his coat to the floor. 'What's the matter?'

'Now his probe circuit's jammed.'

'Oh, that's easy, just waggle his tail.' The Doctor picked up his coat and tossed it carelessly back on the stand.

'All right. We've tried everything else.' Romana waggled K9's tail.

His eyes lit up and his antennae quivered alertly. 'Thank you, Mistress, repairs complete.'

Shoving the electro-pliers in her pocket, Romana straightened up, stretched, and walked over to check the console.

'Well done, Romana,' said the Doctor kindly. 'You're developing a very sound grasp of this kind of high technology.'

'Developing? I was better qualified than you when I arrived!'

The Doctor chose to ignore this. He went over to the table. 'K9, what do you know about the Prion Planetary System?'

K9 chanted metallically, 'There was once an advanced hi-tech society on Zolfa-Thura, a more primitive one on Tigella. Zolfa-Thura destroyed itself in a global war. The planet is

41

now featureless desert.'

'And now only Tigella's left,' said the Doctor thoughtfully. 'With the Dodecahedron . . .'

'Affirmative.'

Suddenly Romana was back at the table, repairing K9. His eyes went dim. 'Oh blast! Here we go again!'

The Doctor tripped over the hat-stand, knocking his coat to the floor. 'What's the matter?'

'Now his probe-circuit's jammed!'

'Oh, that's easy, just waggle his tail' The Doctor picked up his coat, tossed it back on the stand.

'All right, we've tried everything else!' Romana waggled K9's tail.

His eyes lit up and his antennae quivered alertly. 'Thank you, Mistress, repairs complete.'

The Doctor and Romana looked uneasily at each other. Something was very wrong.

Meglos chuckled silently as he watched the repeated sequence on his viewing screen. 'Flies trapped in amber. Not even the Doctor can escape from a chronic hysteresis!'

'A what?' asked Grugger uneasily.

'A time loop. I have the Doctor trapped in a fold in time. All it requires is a little local re-shaping of the continuum.'

'That's good,' said Grugger. 'That's very good!' He didn't really understand what Meglos was saying. What he did understand was that his new partner had a number of very unexpected and dangerous powers. Shape-changing, psychic transference, now time-engineering. Grugger decided to treat Meglos with the utmost caution, and not to betray him until he was sure it would be absolutely safe.

'Makes no sense to me,' grumbled Brotodac.

Meglos was studying the Doctor's face on the screen with peculiar intensity. 'His only respite is the short period before he loops back to the start. Whatever he does he will always return to that point.'

Grugger laughed. 'Round and round, eh? For all eternity!'

'Exactly. An appropriate fate, don't you think, for a Time Lord?' said Meglos. His eyes were still fixed on the Doctor's face.

'Oh blast!' said Romana. 'Here we go again!'

The Doctor tripped over the hat-stand, knocking his coat to the floor. 'What's the matter?'

'Now his probe circuit's jammed!'

'Oh, that's easy, just waggle his tail.' The Doctor picked up his coat and tossed it back on the stand.

'All right, we've tried everything else!' Romana waggled K9's tail.

His eyes lit up and his antennae quivered alertly. 'Thank you, Mistress, repairs complete.'

'That's the third time,' said the Doctor explosively. 'What's happening?'

Romana hurried over to the console and made a rapid check. 'The TARDIS seems to be working normally.'

'Then what is it?' muttered the Doctor.

'Repeated time cycles. It couldn't be a chronic hysteresis, could it?'

Romana was appalled. 'I hope not. If it is, we'll be stuck here forever.'

She was back at the table, repairing K9. 'Oh blast, here we go again!' Under the circumstances her words had a new and ironic meaning.

The Doctor tripped over the hat-stand and his coat fell to the floor. 'What's the matter?'

Meglos was hunched over the viewing screen, his hands fingering his face.

Grugger meanwhile was trying to explain things to Brotodac. A difficult task, since Brotodac's understanding was severely limited, and Grugger himself didn't really know what he was talking about. As Grugger finished his explanation, Brotodac scratched his head, more bemused than ever. 'So this Meglos can bend time?'

'That's right. Bend it right into a loop.'

'I've never heard of that, have you? How's it done?'

'What does it matter how it's done?' asked Grugger, who had very little idea himself. 'The whole point is, the Doctor doesn't get to Tigella.'

'But he does, gentlemen,' said Meglos softly. 'He does!' He pressed a control and for a moment his whole body was bathed in a column of brilliant white light. The light faded, and Meglos swung round to face them. 'We mustn't disappoint the Tigellans!'

Grugger and Brotodac gaped.

The green colouring and the spikes of Meglos

were gone. The features of the Earthling were gone. They were looking into the face of the Doctor.

Meanwhile the Doctor, the real Doctor, was striding up and down the TARDIS, desperately trying to think of some escape. He slammed a fist into his palm. 'It's just no good! Every time we try to –'

Romana was back at the table. 'Oh blast! Here we go again!'

And so they did. Remorselessly, inevitably, the Doctor tripped over the wobbly hat-stand, knocking his coat to the floor. 'What's the matter?'

'Now his probe circuit's jammed.'

'Oh, that's easy, just waggle his tail.' The Doctor picked up his coat and tossed it back on the stand.'

'All right, we've tried everything else!'

Romana waggled K9's tail and once again his eyes lit up and his antennae quivered, and once again he said metallically, 'Thank you, Mistress, repairs complete.'

Romana and the Doctor dashed back to the console. 'Doctor, what can we try now? How can we break it?'

'I'm not sure. Try asking K9.'

Romana ran to the table. 'K9 is there any way out of a chronic hysteresis?'

'Negative, Mistress. No known technological procedure.'

'What about stopping the time rotor, Doctor? There must be something.'

45

'No known technological procedure,' muttered the Doctor. 'No *technological* procedure . . .'

Romana was back at the table. 'Oh blast! Here we go again!'

The Gaztaks watched in astonishment, as Meglos completed the process of transformation. He made a few final adjustments to his height, and the shape of his face. He studied the Doctor's clothes carefully, punched co-ordinates into a machine and disappeared into a cubicle, returning very shortly dressed exactly like the Doctor. He looked at their astonished faces and smiled. '*If* you are ready, gentlemen?'

Pre-setting the controls, Meglos led the way out of the laboratory across the burning sands towards the Gaztak space-ship. As Meglos's laboratory sank slowly into the sand, the Gaztak space-ship lumbered into the skies.

The attack on Tigella had begun.

5

The Double

Meglos spent most of the short journey to Tigella in a disdainful silence.

It was true that General Grugger's space-ship was nothing to enthuse about. It was small and dark and cramped, with a grimy metallic interior. The instruments in the two-man cockpit were almost obsolete, and the only concession to passenger comfort were the rows of hard uncomfortable seats that filled the body of the ship.

Brotodac was at the controls, with Grugger behind. Meglos, now in clothes and appearance an almost perfect replica of the Doctor, sat beside him.

The rows behind them were filled with Grugger's Gaztaks, who sat clutching their strange collection of weapons in phlegmatic silence, neither knowing nor caring where they were going. Soon they would land somewhere, and then they would rob and murder and pillage, just as they always did. That was enough. After all, they were Gaztaks.

The shape of a planet swam up on a murky vision screen. Brotodac pointed. 'Tigella. Ten seconds to atmospheric entry. Activating heat shields.' He thumped a control, and there was a slow grinding of heavy machinery.

'Heat shields,' said Meglos patronisingly. 'What a fascinating vessel this is.'

Grugger caught the sneer in his voice. 'It still works. And without it, you'd still be in your pot on Zolfa-Thura.'

Brotodac turned. 'I've got a fix on the main city entrance. Are we putting down there?'

Frontal attack had never been Grugger's style. 'No. A jungle landfall, a bit to the north.'

'Stand by for landing,' said Brotodac. 'Entering foliage now.'

Flame blazing from its retro-rockets, the Gaztak ship smashed into the jungle like a falling meteor.

In the fluctuating light of the Power Room Annexe, Zastor stood waiting.

After a moment, Lexa came out of the Power Room, her face grave.

'Well, Lexa?' asked Zastor gravely.

Lexa made no reply.

From somewhere in the distance there came the sound of an explosion, followed by faint shouts and cries. Lexa and Zastor both knew that technicians and medical teams would be rushing to deal with yet another crisis. Recently, the power surges had been more frequent than ever before.

Reluctantly Lexa said, 'This Time Lord may visit us.'

'You will allow him to inspect the Dodecahedron?'

48

'On one condition. He must take the Deon Oath.'

'No! That would be an insult to our guest. How can we ask a Time Lord to swear allegiance to Ti, god of Tigella?'

Lexa smiled coldly. 'Another chance for you to impress us all with your diplomacy, Zastor.'

The doors of the Gaztak space-ship slid open, and Meglos, Grugger and Brotodac emerged. They stood in a tiny charred clearing, newly created by the blast of the ship's landing rockets. Outside the little circle of burned foliage, dense impenetrable jungle seemed to press in on them malignantly. Vines and shrubbery and reeds and oddly shaped plants were all crowded together, struggling for survival.

Grugger looked round and shuddered. 'We wait here for one hour then?'

Meglos nodded. 'One hour precisely.'

'Do we come and get you if anything goes wrong?'

Meglos smiled the Doctor's smile, though with none of the humour and warmth. 'If something goes wrong? My dear General, I sometimes think you forget who I am!' He turned and strode away, forcing his way through the jungle as if he expected it to make way for him.

'What a mind,' said Brotodac admiringly. 'I think he could do anything. Anything!'

Grugger didn't care for this hero-worship of their new ally. 'Don't think too hard, Brotodac, you'll burst something.'

Brotodac watched the tall figure disappear into

the jungle. 'I'll tell you something else—I like that coat!'

Once again, Deedrix was busy at Central Control, dealing with the unending flow of crises. Zastor and Lexa looked on. He despatched an emergency team to deal with the latest burn-out, and leaned back wearily. 'When will this Doctor arrive, Zastor?'

'Soon. Very soon.'

'The moment he arrives, I want Caris to bring him here.'

'Having first filled his mind with scientific nonsense I presume,' said Lexa acidly.

'I hope the Doctor will appreciate all our difficulties, Zastor,' said Deedrix pointedly.

Zastor refused to be drawn. 'The Doctor has the maturity to respect many points of view.'

An urgent voice came from the console. 'Temperature rising in food store.'

Deedrix returned to his work.

Caris stood waiting at the City entrance. The entrance itself was a double door in a kind of stone blockhouse in the jungle. Inside, steps led downwards, to the safety of the underground city.

Caris stared hungrily around at the jungle. 'We could inhabit the surface again,' she said fiercely. 'We could! If this Doctor fails us, we may have to!'

There were two black-uniformed City guards flanking the gate. Caris glanced at them to see their reaction, but their faces were impassive. To them Caris's words were blasphemy, and they feared contamination.

There was a rustling in the foliage and a figure stepped out of the jungle, a tall curly-haired man in a long, elegant coat. 'I am the Time Lord, the Doctor,' said Meglos. 'You are expecting me, are you not?'

Caris bowed her head. 'Yes indeed, and you are most welcome. Please follow me.' She led the way into the City.

A panic-stricken voice blared from the console. 'Central storage banks overloading. Shall I close off receptor panels?'

'No,' snapped Deedrix. 'Not yet. Re-route surplus to section five, they have spare capacity.'

Lexa came back into Control. 'Zastor! The preparations for the oath-taking ceremony are complete.'

Deedrix looked up. 'What? You're really going to make him take that ridiculous oath? This is madness, Zastor.'

'It is necessary, Deedrix.'

Caris appeared in the doorway. 'The Time Lord is here.' She stood aside as Meglos, in his Doctor shape, came into the room.

Zastor said eagerly, 'Doctor, it's good to see you again.'

The new arrival stared blankly at him. 'Again?'

A little hurt, Zastor said, 'Of course it has been many years since we met. I must have changed greatly. I am Zastor, now Leader of Tigella.'

'Of course. I remember you well.'

'You've hardly changed at all, Doctor. A little

older, a little wiser, eh?'

'Oh, much wiser, I assure you.' Brusquely dismissing Zastor, he turned to Deedrix. 'I gather your energy source has become a little capricious?'

'Capricious? It's totally out of control.'

'Indeed. You will excuse me?'

Deedrix moved quickly aside, and the visitor took his place at the console, studying the banked rows of instruments. 'You employ some form of energy absorption system I presume?'

'A series of receptor panels, placed above the Dodecahedron. The radiated energy is absorbed and stored.' He pointed. 'It's measured here.'

'The panels can be closed down?'

'The central storage banks will be able to absorb the energy for about one hour. But it's extremely dangerous, of course, and with these fluctuations . . .'

'One hour is all I need. Turn them off.'

Deedrix looked at Zastor, who nodded.

Deedrix flicked a switch and spoke into the console. 'Close down receptor panels until further notice.'

'Excellent! Now take me to the Dodecahedron.'

Zastor waved the distinguished visitor ahead of him. 'After you, Doctor. I'm sure you remember the way.'

The visitor hesitated, then said smoothly. 'You are Leader now, Zastor. I will follow you.'

Lexa stepped forward, barring the way. 'Time Lord! Before entering the Power Room, you must swear allegiance to Ti. You must take the Deon Oath.'

Zastor looked anxiously at the visitor. 'A mere formality, Doctor, but a necessary one.'

'Well, Doctor,' demanded Lexa. 'Will you swear allegiance to Ti?'

It was quite clear what she hoped the answer would be. But she was to be disappointed. 'With the greatest of pleasure. I'd be delighted. Indeed, I am most flattered that you should think me worthy. Will you lead the way?'

Baffled, Lexa led the way from the control room.

Zastor glanced curiously at the Time Lord. Of course, the Doctor was only being diplomatic. But, just for a moment, Zastor had had the distinct impression that his visitor would say or do anything to get inside the Power Room.

'All right, we've tried everything else,' said Romana. She waggled K9's tail.

K9's eyes lit up, and his antennae quivered. 'Thank you, Mistress, repairs complete.'

And once again the Doctor and Romana had a few brief minutes of freedom.

'We can't get out of it,' cried Romana hysterically. 'We've tried everything.'

'That's what you said about repairing K9 –' The Doctor broke off. 'That's it. "We've tried everything." Of course!'

'What?'

'Romana, can you remember the rest of what you said?'

'I should do, we've been through it enough times.'

'That's how we'll get out! We'll throw it out of phase.'

'Go through the sequence deliberately?'

'Exactly. *Before* it comes round again.'

Romana ran to the table. 'Hurry, Doctor, you were over there by the hat-stand.'

'Yes, of course. Right then. Off you go!'

'Oh blast, here we go again,' said Romana brightly.

A little belatedly, the Doctor tripped over the hat-stand, knocking his coat to the floor. 'What's the matter?'

'Now his probe circuit's jammed!'

The Doctor picked up his coat and tossed it onto the stand – and stood looking at Romana with his mouth open. He had forgotten his lines.

Romana pointed frantically at K9's tail and the Doctor said very quickly, 'Oh-that's-easy-just-waggle-his-tail!'

Suddenly time seemed to slow down as the re-enactment fought against the power of the chronic hysteresis.

The Doctor and Romana spoke in slow groaning voices, and moved very, very slowly, as if wading through treacle.

'All ... right ... we've ... tried ... everything ... else,' said Romana laboriously. Very slowly, she waggled K9's tail.

Even more slowly K9 responded. 'Thank ... you ... Mistress ...'

Suddenly time snapped back to normal speed and K9 said crisply, 'Repairs complete.'

'Phase cancellation!' shouted Romana. 'We've done it.'

'Well done,' said the Doctor cheerfully. 'Mind

you, for a moment there, I thought you'd forgotten your lines!'

Meanwhile another Doctor, the Meglos version, was standing on the huge triangular rock in the centre of the Power Room Annexe. There were ominous rusty brown stains around the base of the rock, though no one ever referred to them.

Lexa was standing next to him on the rock, and they were surrounded by purple-robed acolytes bearing blazing torches. 'And never to transgress the laws of the Dodecahedron,' chanted Lexa.

'And never to transgress the Laws of the Dodecahedron,' repeated Meglos obediently.

'Thanks be to Ti,' chanted Lexa.

'Thanks be to Ti,' chanted the assembled Deons.

Zastor, Lexa and Deedrix, who had been watching the ceremony, gave a collective sigh of relief.

Meglos and Lexa stepped down from the rock, and Lexa said majestically, 'You are now free to enter the Power Room, Doctor.'

'Thanks be to Ti,' muttered Deedrix under his breath.

Meglos looked across to the arched doorway of the Power Room. The light that streamed through it was pulsing more erratically than ever. He raised his voice. 'People of Tigella! What I have to do now is extremely dangerous. To control the output of energy it may first be necessary to provoke even more violent emissions.'

Deedrix looked worried. 'Then you'll be in danger yourself?

'Hardly,' said Meglos loftily. 'I am a Time Lord. Having existed in the future, I cannot die in the present.'

'That can't be true, it's a philosophical paradox.'

'No, simply beyond your comprehension.' Meglos raised his voice again. 'However your lives will be in great danger. You must all leave!' A note of exultation came into Meglos's voice. 'I alone – I alone shall enter the Power Room!'

Lexa said angrily. 'It was agreed that I should accompany you, on the god's behalf.'

'I have taken the Deon oath,' Meglos reminded her. 'I now have the protection of Ti. Would you appear to distrust his blessing?'

Defeated by her own weapons, Lexa stepped back. 'So be it.' She raised her hands. 'Leave! All of you leave. No one shall come near till the Doctor is done.'

The TARDIS door opened and the Doctor – the real Doctor – emerged into a jungle clearing, followed by Romana and K9.

The Doctor looked around the dense green wall of jungle. 'According to my calculations, this should be close to the City gate.'

Romana looked around her. 'Well, if this is so close to the City, I can only assume we're in some sort of park, or zoological gardens.'

The Doctor looked at the dense jungle in mild surprise. 'All this greenery has shot up quite a bit since I was last here . . .'

'Where's the City gate, then?'

The Doctor tried to fix his bearings. 'Let me

see . . . I think it has to be . . . this way!' The Doctor set off through the jungle.

K9 however was setting off in the opposite direction. 'Bearing of City, 22 degrees north, 36.4 degrees south.'

'Doctor!' said Romana warningly.

'Ah, yes of course! Anyone can make a mistake.'

They set off after K9.

Alone, Meglos walked into the Power Room, and stood for a moment gazing silently at the Dodecahedron.

The immense five-sided crystal stood on a massive plinth in the centre of the bare rock-walled chamber, filling the whole room with its fiercely pulsing golden light. Above were ranged the great silver receptor panels.

'Ten thousand years,' said Meglos softly. 'Ten thousand years!' He took the L-shaped Re-dimensioner from his pocket, and adjusted its controls. The Re-dimensioner glowed, and gave out a low hum of power. Meglos placed it on the plinth beneath the Dodecahedron. He stepped back – and waited.

6

The Impossible

Led by K9, the Doctor and Romana were trekking through the jungle. 'Listen,' the Doctor was saying, 'I only got the direction wrong because of Tigella's anti-clockwise rotation.'

Romana wasn't listening. She was peering at a patch of charred vegetation. 'Look, K9, these leaves are burned.'

'Partial incineration of vegetation evident,' agreed K9. 'Anomaly.'

'Come on, you two, there's no time for botany,' said the Doctor over his shoulder. 'We're late already!' He strode off through the jungle.

Romana crumbled a charred leaf between her fingers. 'What would cause that, K9? Thinness of the atmosphere?'

'Negative, Mistress.'

'Something to do with this Dodecahedron?'

'Negative. Projection of Dodecahedron pulse insufficient to explain anomaly. Possible cause, retro-rockets of descending space vessel. Come, Mistress.' K9 trundled off after the Doctor.

Romana studied the patch of charred vegetation. There seemed to be a kind of trail of it, with the burning more severe further along, as if it was closer to the source. Curiously, Romana moved forward a little – and a snakelike creeper lashed out and wrapped itself around her foot. She opened her mouth to scream and a bell-like flower swooped down and dropped over her head like a hood. She smelt the sweet fumes of some narcotic gas.

The scientific part of Romana's mind was registering an interesting attack method evolved by the carnivorous plant: one end of it tied up the prey, the other knocked it out. At the same time, the more practical side of her nature led her to struggle frantically until she had wrenched the bell-plant from her head.

Groping in her pocket she produced the electro-pliers she had used on K9 and began snipping at the vine around her feet. It felt as tough as steel cable . . .

Caris moved silently into the deserted Power Room Annexe. Unable to resist the temptation, impelled by scientific curiosity, she had disobeyed the order to stay away. She gasped as a hand fell on her shoulder, and whirled round, astonished to see the tall figure of the high priestess. 'Lexa!'

'What are you doing here, Caris?'

Caris pulled away. 'It is vital that we Savants understand what is going on here.'

'You were ordered to stay away.'

'And so were you, Lexa!'

'I watch on behalf of the god . . . '

Both women turned as they heard footsteps coming from the Power Room. Instinctively, both ducked back into the shadows.

Meglos appeared from the Power Room. His face rapt, and exalted, he stalked past without seeing them, and began climbing the staircase that led to the upper level of the City.

'Did you see his face?' whispered Lexa in awe. 'He communes with the god.'

More practically Caris said, 'What's happened to the light?'

Lexa whirled round and looked at the doorway to the Power Room. For the first time in living memory it was in darkness. The light of the Dodecahedron was gone.

Unaware that they had left Romana behind, the Doctor marched up to the City gate, K9 at his heels.

He went up to the two guards. 'Hello, I'm the Doctor, I believe you're expecting me?'

The guards stared at each other. Then one of them said, 'Greetings, Doctor, I didn't see you go out?'

The Doctor looked puzzled. 'I'm sorry?'

'This is the second time you've been here.'

'Remarkable memory, you must have, old chap. It's been fifty of your years since I was here last. Come along, Romana. Romana?' The Doctor looked down at K9. 'Do you know where she's got to?'

'Yes, Master,' said K9, literal-minded as ever.

'Well, run along and fetch her – and tell her to hurry up! I'd better get on.'

'Master.' K9 turned and trundled back into the jungle.

'My assistant should be along in a moment. Let her through, will you?' With an amiable nod to the baffled guards, the Doctor strode into the City.

Caris and Lexa stood in the darkened Power Room, staring up at the empty plinth.

'It isn't possible,' breathed Caris. 'It just isn't possible.'

Nevertheless, it had happened. The Dodeca-hedron was gone.

It took Romana quite a time to free herself from the bell plants. The vines were incredibly tough, and as soon as she got through one, another took its place. She broke free at last, with a gasp of relief. 'Lush aggressive vegetation!' she said to herself. 'No wonder the Tigellans live underground.'

Romana was about to set off after the Doctor and K9 when something caught her eye. 'More charred vegetation. How very odd. I wonder if it was a ship . . .' Romana hesitated. She knew she ought to hurry and join the Doctor. But then, since he was so confident in his ability to deal with the Tigellans' problem, he could very well manage by himself. She began following the trail of burned vegetation.

In Central Control, Caris and Lexa were telling their incredible story to Deedrix and Zastor.

'We watched the Doctor walk by, I tell you,' said Caris. 'And now the Power Room's empty!'

Deedrix touched a switch. 'Central Control

here. Re-activate receptor panels.' He waited, looking tensely at the energy-intake gauges. Nothing happened.

'It's dead,' said Deedrix unbelievingly. 'There's no power down there.'

'But where is the Doctor?' asked Zastor. 'He didn't come back here.'

'He has betrayed us,' announced Lexa fiercely. 'Out of my way.' Pushing Deedrix aside, she leaned over the console. 'This is Control Command. Arrest the Alien, the Time Lord known as the Doctor. Stop him at all costs. He must not leave the City.'

The announcement echoed through every loudspeaker in the City. It echoed down the walkway along which Meglos was hurrying with long strides. 'This is a Control Command. Arrest the Time Lord. Arrest the Time Lord.'

Faced with the prospect of detection, the iron will of Meglos weakened for a moment. The strain of controlling the Earthling whose body he had taken, and of holding that body in the form of the Doctor was very great.

For a moment the Doctor-face seemed to blur. It changed colour to a cactus-like green, and cactus-spines appeared on hands and face. He heard footsteps coming along the corridor. Panic-stricken Meglos ran for an opening just ahead and ducked inside. He found himself in a hydroponic food bay, where lush green plants were growing in chemical solutions.

He could have found no better hiding place. Feeling strangely comforted, Meglos crouched down amongst the greenery, while the guards ran past in the walkway outside.

In a remarkably short space of time, the Doctor managed to get himself lost amongst the endless identical staircases and walkways. 'That's odd,' he muttered. 'I was sure Central Control was somewhere along here.'

A guard came running along the walkway, and the Doctor turned cheerfully towards him. 'Excuse me, I'm the Doctor. I am expected. I wonder if you could let people know I've arrived.'

The guard covered the Doctor with his blaster, and from somewhere above him a loudspeaker blared, 'Arrest the Doctor! Capture the Time Lord. Stop him at all costs!'

'Very impressive,' said the Doctor thoughtfully. 'Not quite what I had in mind though!'

He heard footsteps and saw two more guards running along the walkway. With them was a tall, angry-looking lady in an imposing head-dress. She looked like some kind of priestess. 'Take him,' she shouted.

The guards grabbed hold of the Doctor's arms.

Sure there was some misunderstanding, the Doctor made no attempt to resist. 'It's all right,' he said soothingly. 'I'm expected here. I'm the Doctor.'

'Where is the Dodecahedron?' demanded the angry woman.

The Doctor sighed. 'I've no idea. I can't even find Central Control.' To his relief, the Doctor saw his old friend Zastor hurrying along the corridor, a good deal older, but as wise and patient-looking as ever. 'Zastor, my dear fellow, I am glad to see you. Would you please tell this lady who I am.'

Zastor seemed to be in a state of some distress. 'What happened, Doctor? Where have you been?'

'Ah yes, so that's it. I'm sorry I'm so late. We would have been here earlier, but we got trapped in a chronic hysteresis—that's a sort of time loop. My assistant will probably be here in a moment, she'll explain everything. Anyway, how are you, Zastor?'

'Baffled, Doctor,' said Zastor sadly. 'I think you'd better come with us.'

Surrounded by guards, the Doctor was marched away.

The trail of burned vegetation grew wider and wider. Since it had been made by the blazing retro-rockets of the Gaztak space-ship, it naturally led Romana to the clearing where the ship itself had landed.

Romana stared at the squat grey shape. 'So that's it . . .' She turned—and found herself looking up at a tall, skeletally thin man. He was dressed in an array of rather tatty-looking military finery, and carried an ugly-looking blaster. 'I do beg your pardon,' said Romana politely.

The grotesque figure made a grab for her, and she turned and ran.

Not far away in the jungle, K9 realised that he

would be unable to complete his mission. 'Mistress? Mistress?' he called pathetically.

There was no reply.

'Batteries require re-charge,' said K9 in a slow, sad, droning voice. 'Must . . . return . . . to . . . City . . . ' He turned and trundled slowly back the way he had come.

Romana ran and ran and ran – but wherever she turned a grotesque military figure reared up ahead of her. Not the same man, she soon realised, but all very similar, all equally villainous-looking.

Like a pack of mangy hounds, the Gaztaks hunted Romana down, containing her in smaller and smaller circles, until she was at last driven back to Brotodac, who stood waiting by the Gaztak space-ship.

Brotodac looked down at her regretfully. Pretty little thing, fetch quite a few credits in the slave markets. Still, they had already accepted one mission, and Brotodac had always prided himself on being a good professional. He turned to the nearest Gaztak. 'She's seen too much. Kill her!'

7

Prisoner of the Gaztaks

As the Gaztaks closed in, Romana retreated until she could retreat no further, her back pressed against the side of the space-ship.

'No, please . . .' she gasped. 'Just listen for a moment . . . '

The Gaztaks raised their weapons in a sort of impromptu firing-squad.

Romana closed her eyes, pressing herself against the side of the ship – and suddenly, miraculously it opened behind her, and she fell against another man, bigger, fatter, uglier and more ornately dressed than all the rest.

Grugger shoved her away from him. He looked at Brotodac. 'Who is she?'

Brotodac shrugged. 'We found her spying on the ship.'

'She's not a Tigellan.' He turned to Romana. 'Where are you from?'

'You wouldn't understand if I told you.'

Grugger grabbed her by the collar with both hands and lifted her till her face was very close to his own. 'Try me!' he suggested.

Romana kicked and struggled. 'Let me go and I'll tell you.'

Grugger dropped her.

'Thank you,' said Romana with dignity. 'If you must know, my ship landed here by mistake. We crashed.'

Grugger looked thoughtful. A crashed space-ship meant only one thing to him. The chance of loot.

Brotodac knew what his leader was thinking. 'Let's just kill her,' he urged. 'Meglos won't like it if we get involved.'

The mention of Meglos clinched matters – in Romana's favour. 'I'm running this expedition,' growled Grugger. 'Not Meglos.' He turned to Romana. 'What kind of ship? Where is it?'

'I'll show you,' said Romana. 'If I can find it.'

Grugger jabbed her with his blaster. 'Move!'

Deedrix stared up at the empty plinth, unable to believe the evidence of his own eyes. The Dodecahedron was gone.

Caris was repeating her story. 'We saw the Doctor leave – and when we came in here, the Dodecahedron was gone!'

'How long was he in here?'

'A matter of minutes. Hardly any time at all.'

Deedrix shook his head. 'It's inconveivable. There's no way I know of that anyone could move an object like the Dodecahedron. Not single-handed.'

'But what was the Dodecahedron?' asked Caris. 'We knew its size and shape and colour, and when it was up there we could monitor the energy output. But what did we really know about it?'

Deedrix shrugged. 'Very little. Over the years we've formed theories . . . '

'The source of our energy,' said Caris bitterly. 'The heart of our civilisation, a device we've become totally dependent upon – and all we have is a few vague theories.'

A group of Deon acolytes had entered the Power Room, and were staring in disbelief at the empty plinth. Their god had deserted them.

Deedrix nodded towards them. 'Yes – and all because of these Deons.'

From the Power Room Annexe they heard the sound of the loudspeaker. 'Central Control to Deedrix. Central Control to Deedrix. Power drain now reaching critical point.'

'The whole City will collapse,' whispered Caris. 'How often have I warned the Chamber . . .'

They huried towards the door. 'I know, I know,' agreed Deedrix. ' "We should all return to the surface." Come on, I'll need you in Control.'

For a moment it looked as if the group of angry, silent Deons would bar their way. They both knew that the Deons would blame the Savants for the loss of the Dodecahedron, that reprisals were more than possible. Caris and Deedrix moved forward steadily.

After a tense moment, the little knot of Deons parted to let them through.

Thankfully, they hurried away.

Romana pointed to the gleam of metal between the foliage. 'There it is!'

Eagerly the Gaztaks bustled her forward.

Suddenly Grugger stopped. He swung round, his face red with anger. 'It's a spacecraft all right! The other side of *our* spacecraft. You're leading us round in circles.'

'Sorry,' said Romana brightly. 'Let's try again.'

'Essential services only,' ordered Deedrix. 'Close down all other sections. I'm reducing lighting, cutting thermostat temperature to minimum.'

Already it was cold and dark in Central Control. There was an atmosphere of impending disaster.

'How long does that give us?' asked Caris.

'About two hours. You'd better hurry up and check those sub-control sections. Quite a lot have been damaged.'

Caris went off and Deedrix turned his attention to the group behind him. Zastor and Lexa were questioning the Doctor, who was listening to the story of his supposed crime.

'Completely disappeared?' asked the Doctor in astonishment. 'Evaporated? As I remember, the Dodecahedron was much too large to move, from what I was told. You never let me see it.'

'Doctor, please,' pleaded Zastor. 'You've paralysed our City.'

'What happened to the Dodecahedron?' demanded Lexa. 'Answer me, Doctor!'

'I keep telling you, I've only just arrived. I don't know what happened.'

'You went into the Power Room. I saw you,' shouted Lexa.

Deedrix came over to them. 'Doctor, whatever

70

reasons you have for doing this, the fact remains that without the Dodecahedron's energy this City will be dead in two hours.'

The Doctor stared wonderingly at Lexa. 'You saw me go into the Power Room? You saw me?'

Once again Romana's back was flattened against the side of the Gaztak space-ship. This time it was Grugger's blaster that threatened her. 'Give me one good reason why I shouldn't kill you now,' he grunted.

'Anti-clockwise rotation,' said Romana rapidly.

'What?'

'I forgot that the planet rotates in an anti-clockwise direction.'

'What's she talking about?' muttered Brotodac. 'Kill her!'

Grugger took the occasion to show off his scientific knowledge. 'It's a question of relative rotational direction. You wouldn't understand.'

'What difference does it make?'

Grugger looked at Romana, who said hurriedly, 'Well, don't you see? If we'd gone the other way we wouldn't keep coming back to this same point!' Romana illustrated this nonsense by drawing mystic circles in the air above her head.

Fortunately for Romana, the Gaztaks, though ferocious, were far from bright. 'Right,' said Grugger heavily. 'I'll give you one last chance. And this time, you'd better get it right.'

They set off once more.

Peering out of his hiding place, Meglos saw that for the moment the corridor was clear.

He was about to move out into the corridor, when suddenly he felt a terrible internal pressure. The personality of the Earthling was struggling to reassert itself. For a moment the features of the Doctor blurred and those of the Earthling took his place. 'Oh no,' snarled Meglos. 'I need you, Earthling.'

Somewhere in his brain, Meglos could actually hear the Earthling's voice. 'Let me go,' it said faintly. 'Let me go, you've no right . . . '

'None at all, Earthling – but the question is academic!' With a mighty effort, Meglos reasserted control. The Earthling's features faded, giving way to those of the Doctor, though the greenish colouring and the cactus spines remained.

The struggle had weakened Meglos, and for a moment he was unable to complete the transformation. Delaying his escape, he sank back into his hiding place.

The Doctor was still protesting his innocence. 'Why don't you find Romana? She'll bear out my story.'

Lexa was scornful. 'Even if this girl exists, her story will prove nothing . . . '

Zastor looked sorrowfully at the Doctor. 'Will you not even admit that you took the Deon oath, and entered the Power Room?'

The Doctor frowned. 'I think I see the problem.'

Deedrix turned away. 'I'll seal off the City. We'll search it, every inch.'

'No, wait,' said the Doctor urgently. 'There are

three possibilities. One, the chronic hysteresis. I've never been in one before and it might have projected a time image of me. It's theoretically possible – I think.'

'And I think you are a fraud and a liar, Doctor,' said Lexa.

'That's the second possibility. But that makes even less sense!'

'Why?'

'Because I simply don't do that sort of thing!'

'And the third possibility?' asked Zastor.

'I think what we've got here is a good old-fashioned *doppelgänger*. A double!'

Close to the cave where Meglos was hiding, there was a sub-control box set into the rock wall. It was one of the sub-units that Caris had come to check. She turned to her accompanying technician. 'I'll deal with this one. You go on to section four food-bays and close down the ray-lamps.'

The assistant went on down the corridor.

Caris opened the control box and began turning down the energy settings. A prickly hand came over her mouth, and dragged her back into the cool green darkness of the hydroponics room.

It was getting colder still in Central Control now, and the lights were dimmer. Deedrix said, 'There's ice forming in some of the sub-corridors. I can't keep even the essential services running for much longer. We'll have to evacuate.'

'One moment,' said Zastor. He turned back to the Doctor. 'I want to trust you, Doctor, but it's hard to doubt my own eyes.'

'Ah, that's the trouble with doppelgangers. You never know who's who!'

Zastor looked at Lexa. She shook her head. 'Confine him. He must not be permitted in the Power Room again.'

For once, Zastor came to a decision. 'No, Lexa, this seems to be the only way. Doctor, we will go to the Power Room together.'

'Let's hope our many hands will make the light work,' said the Doctor brightly, but no one seemed to appreciate the joke.

Zastor and the Doctor left the Control Room.

Lexa stood staring after them, her face dark with anger. 'No, Zastor,' she whispered to herself. 'There is another way!'

Caris stared up at the strange being who was holding her captive. The green colour had gone, the spines disappeared, and to all appearances this was the Time Lord who had come to Tigella such a short time ago. 'Why do you want me to lead you out of the City, Doctor?'

'Precisely because I am not the Doctor!'

'Then who are you?'

'I am Meglos — the last Zolfa-Thuran.' There was a note of fierce pride in the voice, and for just a moment the green colour and the cactus spines seemed to reappear. Then they faded again.

'Zolfa-Thura, the dead planet?'

'Yes!'

'But why should that make me obey you. Why did you come here?'

'For this!' Meglos held out his hand.

74

Caris stared with disbelieving horror at the object he held. 'But that's impossible!'

'Yes,' said Meglos proudly. 'The ultimate impossibility!'

8

The Attack

Lexa had gathered a group of her most devoted acolytes at the bottom of the staircase close to the Power Room. Included in the group were many Deon guards, the military arm of the Deon priesthood. Lexa was talking to them in a low, urgent voice. 'I do not speak in anger, Believers, though we have cause for anger. We will act in justice, in accordance with the ancient custom. Guards, come with me. The rest of you, go and arm yourselves. But do nothing, till I give the word!'

Silently the Deons moved away.

Romana had led her Gaztak captors through the thickest part of the jungle for quite some time now, and they were all looking very much the worse for wear. 'How much more of this, General?' grumbled Brotodac. 'Just look at this jacket.' Brotodac's jacket had been ripped by the razor-sharp thorns – so had Brotodac, though that didn't seem to worry him.

'Shut up,' growled Grugger. He grabbed Romana's shoulder. 'How much further?'

'I don't know,' said Romana plaintively. 'It's

very hard to navigate on a planet that rotates anti-clockwise. I'm pretty certain it's this way – or is it that way?'

Romana stood on tip-toe, looking around her. Suddenly in the distance she saw a patch of very familiar-looking bell flowers. She smiled sunnily up at Grugger. 'Yes, it's this way. Definitely, this way! I recognise those flowers!' She set off through the jungle, trailing her weary captors behind her like an escort.

There was definitely something odd going on, thought Deedrix. He was accompanying the Doctor and Zastor to the Power Room, and all around them there seemed to be a scuffling of silent robed Deons, slipping into the shadows, melting out of sight as you came up to them. What was Lexa up to? And where was Caris?

As the little group headed towards the Power Room, Lexa came hurrying along a walkway, followed by several armed Deon guards. More acolytes appeared from the other direction. 'Follow me,' ordered Lexa. She led them towards the Power Room.

The Doctor stood in the torch-lit Power Room, gazing at the spot where the Dodecahedron had once been.

He scratched his head. 'Assuming some such process as baryon multiplication, the thing would have to be virtually solid . . . '

'We always assumed it would be heavy,' agreed Deedrix.

'Heavy?' said the Doctor. 'At an atomic weight

of around two hundred, not even a dozen of your Tigellans could have carried the thing away.'

'So where is it?'

From the doorway, Lexa said. 'There is no question as to where the Dodecahedron is. It has been taken back by the god.'

Armed Deons were flooding into the Power Room, and the Doctor's Tigellan guards were quickly disarmed.

'What is this, Lexa?' asked Zastor sternly.

'We are taking command,' said Lexa triumphantly. 'In order to pacify the god, all non-believers will be collected and exiled to the surface.'

'But no one can survive up there,' protested Zastor. 'The plants . . . '

'Take them away,' ordered Lexa, and Deon acolytes seized Deedrix and Zastor.

'Lexa, no,' pleaded Zastor. 'You still need my help. You know I have been a Believer all my life.'

'Faith dwells in the deed, Zastor, not the word.' She waved to the guards and Zastor was dragged away.

'He's an old man, Lexa,' shouted Deedrix. 'The plants will kill him.'

His protest was ignored and he too was hurried out.

'How bad are these plants?' asked the Doctor worriedly.

'Most are dangerous,' said Lexa with satisfaction. 'Some are lethal.'

'Really? Well, I'd better hurry then, I've left my companion up there.' The Doctor headed for the door, but the Deons blocked the way.

'You did say all non-believers to the surface?'

'No, Doctor, not you. You are to stay here, and bring us back the Dodecahedron.'

'Well, I'd be delighted to help in the ordinary way . . . '

'You shall help us, Doctor,' said Lexa. 'But not in the ordinary way.'

The guards closed in.

At last Romana had the Gaztaks where she wanted them – in the clearing where the deadly bell-flowers had attacked her not long ago. 'Wait here, a minute,' she said. 'We're nearly there, I recognise this place.'

Brotodac was still unhappy. 'We said we'd wait for Meglos.'

'Stop panicking, he'll make it,' said Grugger carelessly.

'How do we know there is a ship, anyway?'

'If she's lying, she dies,' said Grugger. He jabbed Romana with his blaster.

Romana jumped back. 'Don't do that!' She looked around. 'I know I landed very close to . . . here!' She stamped hard on one of the white vines, and shoved Grugger on top of it. Immediately the vine reared up, winding itself round Grugger, who roared with rage and tried to pull free.

Brotodac went to help him and promptly got entangled himself, as a vine lashed up and coiled round him. Soon all the Gaztaks were struggling with the voracious plants.

Romana meanwhile was haring through the jungle in the direction of the city.

After cutting and slashing and blasting themselves free, Grugger, Brotodac and most of the Gaztaks – one or two didn't make it – came roaring in pursuit.

As Romana neared the City gates, she heard a loudspeaker voice echoing through the jungle. 'Close City exit. Close City exit!'

Romana ran even faster, out-distancing the heavier Gaztaks. She was almost at the gates when she stumbled over something metallic, half-hidden in long grass, 'K9!'

Feebly K9 twitched his tail. 'Mistress!'

Romana realised his batteries had run down.

She looked behind her, and heard the pursuing Gaztaks crashing through the jungle. 'Come on, K9, I can't leave you here.' Heaving him up in her arms, she stumbled towards the gates, which were slowly closing. With a last desperate effort, Romana carried K9 through the fast-closing gap. As the first of the Gaztaks staggered up, the outer door slid shut.

Unfortunately for Romana, the inner doors closed too – leaving her trapped with K9 in the narrow space between.

Gasping for breath, Grugger and Brotodac stood glowering at the closed doors. 'What do we do?' asked Brotodac gloomily.

Grugger's military pride was hurt. 'Attack! We're going in!' Drawing his blaster, he blazed away at the door.

Nothing happened.

Grugger beckoned to two of his men. 'You two. Cut down that tree!'

'You can't get out now,' said Caris. 'They've sealed the exit.'

They had heard the announcements as they made their way to the upper levels.

'Then we must change our plans,' said Meglos. 'There should be a ventilation shaft on the next level.'

'That won't be any good to you either. We closed down all the shafts to preserve heat.'

'You're lying, of course.'

'You're trapped,' said Caris. 'We're all trapped, now that Lexa is in control.'

'We'll head for the main entrance. No one can stop me!'

Inside his head a voice said, 'Are you sure?'

'*Earthling?*' hissed Meglos. '*You again?*'

Ordinary and everyday as he was, George Morris, the Earthling as Meglos called him, had unexpected reserves of strength and courage. He didn't really know what was happening around him, but on some level he was sure that his body and his soul had been invaded, taken over by some alien force. He was fighting for survival – and he brought Meglos to the very edge of defeat.

Astonished and fearful, Caris watched the terrifying internal battle.

The green hue returned to Meglos's skin, and the cactus spines reappeared. 'It is no use,' snarled Meglos. The struggle went on. 'Let go, Earthling, let go. You cannot escape. It will kill you.'

'Nothing could be worse than this,' said the ghostly voice.

'What? A hero and a fool? You are a dangerous combination, Earthling.'

The whole form of Meglos blurred, and the astonished Caris saw the form of a stranger – Morris, though she did not know it – superimposed on the shape of a giant plant. . .

With a supreme effort of will, Meglos reasserted his control. The shape of the Earthling blurred, became green and cactus-like, and was finally transformed into that of the Doctor, apparently normal again, the green colour and cactus spines gone.

Exhausted by the struggle, Meglos drew a deep breath, and found himself facing the end of a power tool, snatched from Caris's work-belt. It was a laser-cutter, designed for shearing through sheet metal – but at close range it made a formidable weapon.

'Whoever you are, or whatever you are,' said Caris steadily. 'You're coming with me.'

Four of the brawniest Gaztaks staggered towards the City door, supporting a massive sharpened tree-trunk between them.

Brotodac yelled, 'Come on lads!'

They smashed the battering-ram against the point where the sliding doors joined, and the doors buckled, just a little.

'Again,' yelled Grugger. 'Again!'

The Gaztaks returned to the attack.

Inside the inner door, the one behind which Romana was still trapped, a group of City guards listened in horror to the sound of the battering ram.

The senior guard ordered. 'Into position. Prepare to fire!'

The guards aimed their blasters at the inner door.

The point of the battering ram thrust through the outer door, narrowly missing Romana who leapt back just in time.

The battering ram was pulled back, then thrust through again, as the Gaztaks returned to the attack. Again it was pulled back. Romana saw that at the next assault, the outer doors would buckle and fly open.

The battering ram smashed forwards again. At that precise moment, the inner doors behind Romana slid open, revealing a line of Tigellan guards with levelled blasters.

Romana threw herself flat as the blaster fire sizzled over her head.

'Out of the way!' shouted the senior guard. 'Pull her clear!'

Romana caught hold of K9 as the guards grabbed her by the feet and dragged both of them inside the City.

Romana pulled K9 out of the line of fire and tucked him into an alcove, just to one side of the doors. 'Stay there, K9, I'll see if there's somewhere to recharge you.'

One final smashing blow of the battering ram broke down the doors at last, and the triumphant Gaztaks poured through – to be met by a hail of Tigellan blaster-fire.

'Get help,' shouted the senior guard. 'City guards, Deons, anyone you can find. Tell them the City's under attack!'

One of the guards turned and dashed away.

The rest of the guards, outnumbered as they were, took up positions and settled down to fight off the invaders.

Haring along the walkway that led away from the gate Romana saw, as she thought, the Doctor hurrying towards her — with a girl holding some kind of weapon on him.

Romana flattened herself into an alcove, let the Doctor go past, and then leapt on his captor from behind.

Hearing the struggle behind him, Meglos turned, and saw Caris and Romana fighting furiously for possession of the laser cutter. Guessing what had happened he walked on clamly towards the shattered gates.

When he arrived the battle was going in the Gaztaks' favour. Most of the City guards had been shot down and the survivors had pulled back to defensive positions inside the City. Here and there Gaztaks were busy looting the dead.

Meglos walked calmly past them and crossing the battleground headed for the jungle. Just outside, Grugger and Brotodac could be seen, directing the attack. They greeted Meglos with wild delight, laughing and shouting.

Romana saw what was happening, and called, 'Doctor, what are you doing?'

Caris struggled to her feet. 'That wasn't the Doctor!'

Romana stared at her. 'What?'

'Come with me,' said Caris wearily. 'I'll explain.'

She led Romana away.

As they moved away from the gate they saw a considerable force of guards, Deons and City guards combined, rushing towards the battle. Reinforcements had arrived.

In the jungle outside the City, Meglos smiled and said ironically, 'Well, gentlemen?'

Brotodac said, 'Isn't he a marvel? He told us to wait for one hour. We attack the City gates instead, and one hour later he strolls out, cool as you please!'

'Shut up, Brotodac,' snarled Grugger. He was watching the battle with a shrewd and experienced eye. The sound of blaster fire from the gates was heavier, more concentrated. 'They've brought up reinforcements. Time to pull back. Brotodac, organise a rearguard in force. Tell them to hold their ground at all costs. It'll give us time to get away!'

Grugger turned to Meglos. 'Well, what happened? Looks as if this whole thing is a catastrophe. Attack beaten off, no Dodecahedron.'

'Let me show you something, General,' said Meglos.

'The Dodecahedron for instance?' sneered Grugger.

'Precisely!' Meglos held out his hand, as he had done to Caris earlier.

In it lay the Dodecahedron, reduced by the

Re-dimensioner to five centimetres in all dimensions.

Brotodac, returned from giving his orders, stared at him in frank admiration. 'How did you do that?'

'He'd never have managed it without me,' said Grugger sulkily.

Meglos laughed. 'I assure you, gentlemen, this is only the beginning!'

9

The Sacrifice

The Annexe to the Power Room was packed full with chanting, exalted Deons, their red and purple robes and ornate head-dresses glinting in the light of the blazing torches that lined the walls.

Lexa was addressing her congregation. 'We must have faith, Deons, faith!'

'Ti! Ti! Ti!' chanted the Deons.

'We can restore the Dodecahedron,' shouted Lexa.

Again the sonorous chant rolled out. 'Ti! Ti! Ti!'

Lexa raised her hand, and the room fell silent. 'We can restore the Dodecahedron, by offering the angry god a sacrifice.' She pointed dramatically. 'A sacrifice for its return. His life, in return for the Great Light that illumines us all!'

'Ti! Ti! Ti!' chanted the Deons.

The Doctor lay spreadeagled on the floor surrounded by the fanatically chanting crowd. He stared at the ceiling high above him, and reflected that, although it wasn't the first sacrifice he had ever been prepared for, it was quite certainly the nastiest.

Triumphantly the surviving handful of Gaztaks marched back through the jungle, leaving the sound of blaster-fire behind them.

After all, they'd sacked a City . . . well, a City gate at least. And they'd looted and pillaged . . . if you could dignify stealing from the pockets of a few dead guards and their own dead comrades with such grandiose terms. Anyway, they'd seen a bit of action and come off more or less victorious, and they were still alive, even if most of their fellows were doomed. Still, that was their bad luck.

They reached the space-ship at last and piled aboard. This time Grugger took the controls. As the last Gaztak came on board, Brotodac fired a few shots towards the City. 'We've done it!' he yelled. 'We've done it! A complete success!'

'We're about to take off, Brotodac,' said Grugger drily. 'If you intend to come with us, I suggest you get in and close the door!'

Brotodac slammed the door and hurried inside. He sat down beside Meglos, and gazed admiringly at him.

Even Meglos was not unmoved by such frank admiration in his hour of triumph. 'Well done, Brotodac,' he said kindly. 'Destination, Zolfa-Thura, I think, General Grugger.'

Grugger began preparations for take-off. 'I hope it's all been worth it, Meglos.'

Meglos looked at the tattered figure of Brotodac in the next seat, and then at the glowing Dodecahedron. 'Oh I think you'll find this will be well worth the odd torn jacket!'

A slightly hysterical voice was squawking from

90

the City loudspeakers. 'The Doctor has escaped. The City doors have been breached. All guards to the gate immediately.'

Romana was listening to Caris's story as they hurried along the walkway. Most of it seemed to make very little sense, but she seized eagerly on the central point. 'So that definitely wasn't the Doctor I saw with you, it was this Meglos creature, this cactus thing impersonating him?'

'That's right. He told me himself, he wasn't the Doctor.'

'Then where is the Doctor? The real one, I mean?'

'I've no idea. You're sure he's here?'

'Positive.'

'Then we'd better try and find him.'

The two girls hurried on their way.

'O, great god of Ti,' chanted Lexa. 'We offer you this sacrifice, and beseech you to restore the Dodecahedron once more to shine in Tigella. Thanks be to Ti!'

'Thanks be to Ti!' echoed the assembled Deons.

Above the spreadeagled Doctor – exactly above the Doctor – the massive triangular rock that had once stood in the centre of the room was now suspended from the high ceiling. It was held in place by three ropes, one from each corner. The ropes were fed over a pulley wheel and then down to the base of the room where they separated again and were anchored to the ground by three ring bolts some distance apart. All three ropes were drawn quiveringly taut by the weight of the enormous rock.

Lexa raised her hand in signal, and an acolyte held a blazing torch to the first of the three ropes.

Quite an inventive idea, thought the Doctor. When the first rope parted, the rock would be supported by two, and when the next one parted, it would hang precariously by one. A rope which might or might not break anyway, but would snap very quickly when they used the torch. And when that went, the rock would come smashing down, pulverising the Doctor, a sacrifice to Ti.

The first rope smouldered through and snapped. The two remaining ropes quivered tautly as they took the strain.

The acolyte with the torch moved over to the second rope. It began to smoulder . . .

Zastor and Deedrix were being herded up towards the City Gate by two Deon guards, when they ran into Caris and Romana, going in the other direction. Caris ran eagerly up to Zastor. 'Your friend the Doctor is innocent! There is another alien, called Meglos, from Zolfa-Thura. He took the Doctor's shape and stole the Dodecahedron.' She caught hold of Deedrix's hands. 'He miniaturised it, Deedrix. I saw it. He held the Dodecahedron in his hand.'

'Then the Doctor was right – the real Doctor, I mean,' said Deedrix, hugging her. 'He said there was a *doppelgänger*!'

Romana looked at the two Deon guards. 'Shouldn't you two be at the Gate? The City's under attack.'

Zastor was horrified. 'The City attacked? By whom?'

'They call themselves Gaztaks. I ran into them on the surface, a whole space-ship full of them, armed to the teeth and vicious. They were giving your guards a pretty bad time when I left.'

Zastor turned to the astonished Deon guards. 'You heard her. Go where you are needed.'

'Lexa's orders—'

'Is Lexa Leader on Tigella or am I?' thundered Zastor. 'Go!'

The astonished guards went.

'Do you know where the Doctor is?' asked Romana.

'The Doctor!' gasped Zastor. 'Lexa took him for sacrifice. I pray we shall be in time.' He led them towards the Power Room at a run.

10

The Reprieve

Two of the rock's supporting ropes had gone by the time Romana and the others reached the Power Room Annexe. Twisting slowly, the great stone was hanging by the last rope, which seemed to be taking the strain – just – though it was stretched to breaking point. Then the acolyte with the torch approached . . .

At least it would be quick, thought the Doctor. With the tension on that rope, it would snap almost as soon as it was touched by the flame.

The acolyte raised the torch . . .

'Stop!'

Lexa and the rest of the Deons turned, to see Zastor standing in the doorway, flanked by Romana and Caris. 'Stop the sacrifice!'

'Heretic!' shrieked Lexa. 'Take him!'

'You've got the wrong Doctor!' shouted Romana. Her eyes were fixed on the one terrifyingly thin rope holding the great rock above the Doctor's body.

'That's right,' confirmed Caris. 'There are two of them, and the other one has just escaped through the City gate. I saw him.'

Lexa would not listen. 'Go! All of you. You are forbidden here.'

'I believe them, Lexa,' said Zastor. 'There really are two Doctors.'

'Lies! More lies!'

A Deon guard, one of those who had been involved in the recent fighting at the gate, ran into the Power Room. 'The Gaztaks have withdrawn,' he announced proudly. 'Most have fled from the gate, and the rest are dead . . .' He broke off, staring in utter astonishment at the Doctor.

'Then the man you want has gone with them,' said Deedrix.

Caris noticed the expression on the face of the guard. 'It's true, isn't it?' she asked. 'A man, exactly like this one, allied with the Gaztaks, escaping with them? You were there, you saw it?'

'Is it true?' demanded Lexa. 'Did you see this other Doctor?'

The guard was standing open-mouthed, his eyes on the Doctor.

The rope holding the rock creaked ominously.

'Please say yes,' said the Doctor calmly.

Slowly the guard nodded. 'Yes . . . it is the truth. I saw the man myself. He left with the retreating Gaztaks . . .'

Romana was already struggling with the Doctor's bonds.

The Gaztak ship was under way and on course for Zolfa-Thura. Grugger was at the controls, Brotodac and Meglos in the seats behind him. Behind them, the few surviving Gaztaks were dressing their wounds, checking their weapons and squabbling over the loot taken from the dead guards, and from their own dead comrades.

Grugger was in a savage mood. 'I lost most of my men on Tigella, Meglos.' He nodded over his shoulder. 'You see what's left?'

'The price of success, General,' said Meglos blandly.

'A price we Gaztaks paid,' Meglos. You could never have escaped if it wasn't for us.'

'You'll be rewarded, all of you. Rulers of the galaxy, all the wealth and power you can imagine.'

Brotodac, essentially a simple soul, liked loot he could see and touch. He was staring wistfully at the coat Meglos was wearing.

Grugger rose and stretched. 'Take over, Brotodac.'

Brotodac took the controls and Grugger slumped into the seat beside Meglos. 'One day I'll go back to Tigella with an army.'

Meglos produced the miniaturised Dodeca-hedron, glowing bright and golden in the gloom of the Gaztak ship. 'Armies are unnecessary – with this. It contains all the power we need to make ourselves obeyed by any planet in the galaxy. So far its potential has hardly been touched.'

'Approaching Zolfa-Thura,' warned Brotodac.

Grugger looked cunningly at Meglos. 'And approaching full potential, eh? When we get back to Zolfa-Thura, you're going to put that thing's power to use?'

'Precisely,' said Meglos, his eyes staring into the glowing depths of the Dodecahedron. 'Precisely!'

Caris was telling the Doctor the story of her encounter with Meglos. 'I saw it, Doctor,' she repeated. 'He was holding the Dodecahedron in his hand.'

'A relatively simple matter of re-dimensional engineering. Did this Meglos say what he wanted with it?'

'He talked about taking it back with him, back to Zolfa-Thura. He said he was the last surviving Zolfa-Thuran.'

'To Zolfa-Thura?' The Doctor rubbed the chafe-marks on his wrists. 'Now why would he want to do that?'

'According to the history books, there's nothing on Zolfa-Thura but sand,' said Romana. 'And the Screens, of course.'

'Screens? What Screens?'

'The Screens of Zolfa-Thura.'

'Did your history books say how many there were?'

'Five, I think. Does it matter?'

'It might. Five Screens, and a five-sided Dodecahedron.' The Doctor rubbed his chin. 'The Screens of Zolfa-Thura. We must go there at once!'

Night was falling on Zolfa-Thura when they arrived. The Gaztak space-ship landed in much the same spot as before, and now Grugger and Brotodac stood watching as Meglos paced up and down in the bare sandy waste between the Screens.

Brotodac, as always, was fascinated by anything Meglos did. 'What's he doing?'

They saw Meglos pacing off distances between the Screens, checking and re-checking measurements and bearings. Finally he stooped, and thrust the Dodecahedron deep into the sand. 'He's buried it,' said Brotodac disappointedly. 'What's he up to?'

'Hmm,' said Grugger judiciously. 'You'll see!' He didn't have the slightest idea.

Brotodac glanced nervously at Meglos and whispered, 'Will he really give it to me, do you think?'

'What?' Then Grugger realised. 'Oh, the coat? Why? Not cold are you?'

'It's such a good coat,' said Brotodac yearningly. 'A wonderful coat. And now he's finished playing the Doctor, he doesn't need it any more.'

He fell silent as Meglos strode towards them. 'Well, gentlemen, we are ready?'

'What happens now?' asked Grugger, a little apprehensively.

'Activation!'

Meglos produced the L-shaped Re-dimensioner from his pocket and adjusted its controls. The Re-dimensioner began humming with power.

Brotodac looked on, with the simple pleasure of a child watching a favourite magician perform a conjuring trick.

As conjuring tricks go, this was a pretty good one. Meglos's laboratory rose once more out of the sand, but this time the glowing Dodecahedron was on top of it. As the laboratory rose, the Dodecahedron grew, returning with amazing speed to its full, impressive size. When the laboratory was fully emerged from the sands, the Dodecahedron was crowning the little tower on top

99

of it, obviously occupying the place for which it had been made. It lit up the night sky like an elaborate lighthouse.

Meglos made more adjustments to the Re-dimensioner, and soon the Dodecahedron was sending out five separate and distinct beams of light, one to each of the five Screens.

Grugger and Brotodac, their faces bathed in the golden light from the beams, stared upwards in utter amazement.

'Come,' said Meglos.

With difficulty, Grugger tore his gaze away from the extraordinary spectacle. 'What happens now?'

'Now we see if it works,' said Meglos. He led the way to his laboratory.

Outside the smashed-in City exit, there was a scene of ruin and devastation. There were dead bodies everywhere, bodies of the Savant and Deon guards, united in death, who had given their lives in the defence of the City. And bodies of the hard-fighting Gaztak rearguard, who had sacrificed themselves so their leaders could escape.

Zastor and Lexa had come to escort the Doctor and Romana from the City.

The Doctor looked round sadly at the scene of carnage. 'Come along Romana, we must hurry.'

Zastor shook him warmly by the hand. 'Good luck on Zolfa-Thura, Doctor.'

And Lexa said, 'Please Doctor, bring the Dodecahedron back to us if you can.'

'I'll try—but it may not be possible. You'd

better start making plans for living without it. It's really not so bad up here after all, you know.'

'If you avoid the bell-plants,' said Romana. Suddenly she remembered. 'K9, I left him just beside the Gate when he ran down. I'll go and get him. We can re-charge him in the TARDIS.'

As Romana ran back towards the City Gates, the flash of movement caught the blurring eyes of one of the fallen Gaztaks, a Gaztak who was wounded, but far from dead. Recovering consciousness to find himself surrounded by victorious Tigellans, he was shamming dead, waiting for a chance to escape in the darkness. At the sight of Romana, his eyes gleamed with hatred. There was the girl! The one who had tricked them and led them wandering through the jungle. It it hadn't been for her, they would never have made that disastrous attack on the City gate. Raising himself painfully on one elbow, he aimed his blaster at Romana's back.

Only Lexa saw what was happening. 'Romana!' she called. 'Look out!' Lexa ran in front of the Gaztak just as he fired. The blaster-beam caught her full in the chest, slamming her to the ground.

Deedrix threw himself down, snatched up a weapon from a dead guard, rolled over and blasted the Gaztak before he could fire again.

Zastor was kneeling beside Lexa. 'She's dead,' he said disbelievingly.

Romana came running back to them. She stopped, shocked and horror-struck at the sight of Lexa's body. 'She saved my life.'

'Yes, she did,' said the Doctor gently. 'But we've got a lot to do, Romana, and other lives to save. Go and get K9, and we'll be on our way.'

'I'm coming with you,' said Deedrix suddenly.

'And me,' said Caris.

The Doctor looked hard at them. 'I don't mind admitting I'll be glad of your help. But it will be dangerous, very dangerous.'

'You're facing danger for us, Doctor,' said Caris. 'The least we can do is share it with you.'

Romana came back carrying K9, who wagged his tail feebly at the sight of the Doctor.

The Doctor patted him on the head. 'We'll soon have you re-charged and fit, old fellow. Come on all of you.'

The little group hurried away into the jungle, leaving Zastor kneeling beside the body of the woman who had been his fiercest opponent and his oldest friend.

When he looked up, the Doctor and his friends were gone – on their way to Zolfa-Thura and the final confrontation with Meglos.

11

The Ultimate Weapon

Meglos was working at his main control console, with Grugger and Brotodac looking on. Both were watching Meglos's every move, Brotodac out of simple fascination and admiration, Grugger for a very different reason, all his own.

Meglos was in an expansive and talkative mood, and he had been favouring them with an account of the history of the Dodecahedron.

It appeared that the Zolfa-Thurans, strange cactoid inhabitants of this desert planet, had been scientists of a particularly brilliant kind. They had escaped the limitations of their vegetable bodies by developing the ability to take over the bodies of other creatures and mould them to their desires. This enabled them to travel the galaxy, disguised as members of any species they might encounter.

'Why did you want us to bring you an Earthling?' asked Grugger, his cunning little eyes following every movement of Meglos's hands.

'I needed a body I could not only control, but re-shape to my will. Experience has shown that the inhabitants of Earth are particularly malleable – most of them at least!' Meglos smiled wryly. 'As it happened you chose a particularly difficult specimen. He gave me a good deal of trouble, though I have him under control now.'

'Why did you want him at all?' persisted Grugger. 'You couldn't have known the Doctor was coming when you sent us the message.'

'My original thought was that I would have to disguise myself as a Tigellan, possibly several Tigellans in quick succession, to gain access to the Dodecahedron. Then I intercepted the Doctor's message and that old fool Zastor's reply. He was actually asking the Doctor to come and examine the Dodecahedron.' Meglos smiled. 'I immediately decided to impersonate the Doctor. Not only did he provide easy access to my goal, but a ready-made scapegoat, to help cover my escape! I imagine the unfortunate Doctor has been flattened by now. A distressingly primitive people, the Tigellans, in many ways, particularly those Deons.' Meglos rubbed his chin in a very Doctor-like gesture. 'I think I'll wear this shape for a while – after all, the Doctor has no further need of it.'

'What happens to the original shape, the Earthling?'

'Oh, he'll die before long, I expect,' said Meglos carelessly. 'The process is very wearing on the host body.'

Grugger looked curiously at him. 'What'll you do then?'

'Revert to my original cactoid shape for a while. This laboratory is adapted to it. Most of its functions can be operated simply by thought-waves – like the doors, for instance.'

'But not what you're doing now?'

'No, more complex operations need manual capabilities. Why do you ask?'

Grugger looked shifty, remembering his original attempt to double-cross Meglos. He was planning a fresh bit of treachery now, though he was determined this one would succeed. It was practically a matter of honour with a Gaztak to double-cross his associates. 'Oh, no reason, just curious.' Uneasily, Grugger wondered if Meglos suspected him. Too conceited, he decided. Meglos was sure he was on top now, and probably convinced Grugger regarded him with the same unthinking adoration as that idiot Brotodac.

'After all,' Meglos said mockingly. 'If I need a new host body you can always provide it!'

Instinctively Grugger stepped back, and Meglos chuckled. 'Don't worry, General, nothing would persuade me to merge with a Gaztak.'

Grugger decided to ignore the insult – for the moment. 'What about this Dodecahedron thing, then?'

Meglos launched into a long account of the Dodecahedron's history. It had been developed by Zolfa-Thura's leading energy-scientists, originally just as a power-source. Then others had realised its supreme potential as a weapon. 'That's when the Screens were built,' said Meglos. 'I designed the weapon myself!'

'So what went wrong?'

Meglos explained that the planet had split into two warring factions. One wanted to preserve the Dodecahedron simply as a power source, another wanted to use the weapon to make their obscure desert planet the supreme ruler of the galaxy. A terrible war had broken out, which had reduced the planet to ruins. Only Meglos himself had survived, hidden in his underground laboratory. Meglos and one other, at least for a while.

The leader of the peace party had stolen the Dodecahedron and fled with it to Tigella. His ship had crash-landed in the jungle, killing him in the process.

'The primitive Tigellans found the Dodecahedron in the jungle, decided it was a gift from the gods, and took it back to their underground city. At first they were content to worship it, though later they developed enough of a technology to use it as a simple power-source . . .'

Meanwhile, in his underground laboratory, Meglos had watched and waited, planning the Dodecahedron's recovery.

'Took your time about it, didn't you?' growled Grugger. 'Ten thousand years!'

'We xerophytes are a long-lived species,' replied Meglos chillingly. 'We can afford to wait.' He straightened up and stepped back from the console. 'Success is all the sweeter for the delay. Some of my fellow Zolfa-Thurans tried to destroy all we had and all we knew to prevent this moment!'

'The Screens are absorbing the power, right?' said Grugger.

Meglos glanced at him in faint surprise. 'Correct, General. Absorbing it, magnifying it, concentrating it. The five beams they throw out can be made to concentrate on any planet in the galaxy.'

106

Even Brotodac could follow this. 'And blast it?'

'To infinitesimal dust!' Meglos smiled. 'Brotodac, you're a discerning sort of fellow. Choose a planet – any planet.'

Brotodac looked helplessly at him. He would happily destroy a space-ship or a city, but an entire planet? The scale was too huge for him. He turned appealingly to Grugger. 'You tell him.'

'Oh, make up your own mind for a change.'

Brotodac thought hard and then gave up. 'It's very good of you, giving me a choice and that, but I'd sooner just have that coat!'

Meglos smiled. 'All right then, General Grugger, it's up to you. What's your choice?'

Grugger still hadn't forgotten his defeat. 'Tigella,' he said instantly. 'Let's start with Tigella!'

The TARDIS materialised some way behind one of the Screens, just outside the circle of light cast by the blazing Dodecahedron. The Doctor, Romana, Caris, Deedrix and a re-charged K9 all emerged and stood looking about them.

Romana patted the TARDIS. 'Well done, we're very close.'

She caught the Doctor's eye and snatched back her hand. She was always reproving the Doctor for treating the TARDIS as a person. Obviously it was catching.

Deedrix was staring up at the blazing glow beyond the Screen. 'It's lighting up the whole sky!'

'Right,' said the Doctor. 'All you lot had better stay here.'

'Where are you going, Doctor?' asked Caris.

'To settle with Meglos, of course.'

'You can't go alone, Doctor,' said Romana. 'There are still quite a few Gaztaks left, and they'll kill you on sight.'

'On sight?' The Doctor smiled. 'That's just what they won't do!'

Romana frowned. 'Why ever not?' Suddenly she understood. 'If they see you, they'll think you're Meglos, at least for a while.'

'Exactly. If Meglos can impersonate me—'

'You can impersonate him!'

'Exactly! Right then, I won't be long.' The Doctor slipped away.

Grugger watched with hawk-like concentration, as Meglos worked on his control settings.

'A final adjustment for relative motion,' said Meglos. He twisted a control and stepped back. 'Well, gentlemen, the beams are now programmed to converge on Tigella.'

'Let's start the countdown,' said Brotodac, who had become quite keen on the idea. He hadn't cared much for Tigella either; those jungle thorns had ruined his coat. 'Will we be able to see it blow up from here?'

'Patience,' said Meglos. He started to slip out of his coat, and Brotodac sprang forward to help him. Rolling up his sleeves, Meglos said, 'We are about to release a power many orders of magnitude greater than any intelligence has hitherto controlled. There can be no room for error. I must go outside and re-check the alignment of the Screens.' Meglos strode outside in his shirt-sleeves, followed by an attendant Gaztak.

Brotodac watched him go, clutching the coat lovingly to his tattered chest.

Moving quietly thorugh the night, the Doctor eventually reached the Gaztak spacecraft. He flattened himself against it as two patrolling Gaztaks went by, but their attention was fixed on the Dodecahedron and they failed to see him. He moved on to the nearest of the Screens.

Peering round the edge, the Doctor saw Meglos come out of the laboratory, and head for one of the other Screens.

'Shirt-sleeves, eh?' said the Doctor, and began slipping out of his coat.

To his horror he felt two hands helping him. He looked over his shoulder and saw a particularly villainous-looking Gaztak, grinning amiably at him. With a sigh of relief, the Doctor realised that his impersonation was working already. The fellow thought he was Meglos.

'Thank you very much,' said the Doctor politely. 'Do you think you could do something else for me?'

The Gaztak nodded.

'Well, the thing is, I'm not sure if this Screen is quite vertical? Would you say it was vertical? Anyway, if you wouldn't mind just holding it for a while, while I check the other side? Let me show you!'

The Doctor positioned the Gaztak so that he was standing, arms stretched upwards, supporting, quite unnecessarily, the lower part of the great metal Screen, the Doctor's coat still clutched in one hand.

'Splendid,' said the Doctor. 'Don't move!'
He hurried away.

Brotodac was shaking the creases out of Meglos's coat. He held it up admiringly. 'Beautiful!'

Grugger looked narrowly at him. He still needed Brotodac, especially with his fighting force cut down to a handful. But could he trust him, when the great bony fool was so dazzled by Meglos? Maybe the coat was the key.

'Put it on,' suggested Grugger.

Brotodac's eyes lit up. Then he shook his head. 'What will he say?'

'Doesn't matter what he says any more,' said Grugger. 'He's talked too much for his own good.' He squinted at Brotodac to see how he was taking all this. Grugger slapped the main console with careless confidence. 'I watched everything he was doing, got him to explain things, you saw?'

'So?'

'So I've got all this all figured out. We don't need him any more. Put the coat on.' Grugger waited tensely. If Brotodac put the coat on – it would mark the end of his loyalty to Meglos – and the end of Meglos as well.

Unable to resist it, Brotodac slipped his arms in the sleeves, shrugged his shoulders into it. He was admiring his own reflection in one of the vision screens when Meglos walked back into the laboratory. Brotodac started guiltily.

Actually it wasn't Meglos at all, it was the Doctor himself, but to Brotodac and Grugger, of course, it was still Meglos.

The Doctor beamed at Brotodac. 'I say, I like

110

you in that coat. Looks well on you.' He hurried over to the main console. 'Now let me see, what have we here?' The Doctor began making rapid alterations to Meglos's control settings.

'What about the countdown?' asked Brotodac.

'Not just yet,' said the Doctor absently. He changed a few more settings.

Grugger looked hard at him, sensing more than suspecting that something was wrong. 'You said it was already programmed.'

'Programmed?'

'To annihilate Tigella.'

'Well, yes it is – nearly,' said the Doctor vaguely. 'Just a few minor adjustments.' He peered at a wheel-like control. 'Now I wonder what that's for?'

'You told me it was for focusing the beams,' said Grugger suspiciously. Meglos was acting very strangely. Was he planning some treachery himself?

'Of course it is, of course it is,' said the Doctor, his fingers flying over the console. 'I must just pop outside for a moment . . .'

The Doctor was just about to leave when a Gaztak entered and handed him his coat. It was the Gaztak the Doctor had left holding up the Screen. Eventually growing bored with this, the Gaztak had moved away, then realised he was still carrying the coat – Meglos's coat, as he naturally thought. In a well-meaning attempt to be helpful he had brought the coat back to its owner.

Grugger looked at the coat in the Doctor's hands, and then looked at the identical coat on

Brotodac's back. 'Two coats?' he said slowly. '*Two coats?* What's going on?'

Meglos finished checking the Screen, and looked at the uncomprehending Gaztak beside him. Grugger had given orders that Meglos was to go nowhere without a Gaztak guard – 'For his own safety'.

'Excellent! The magnification levels are constant. One more check and we are ready to go.'

They moved away.

Romana was waiting by the TARDIS, and getting increasingly worried about the Doctor.

Caris and Deedrix were with her, absorbed in the wonder of the glowing Dodecahedron.

'It's unbelievable,' said Deedrix. 'Just unbelievable.'

Caris said wistfully. 'I'd love to have a closer look.'

'Perhaps we all should,' said Romana crisply. 'Come along K9.'

'Mistress.'

They headed towards the pulsing light.

With a beaming smile, the Doctor held out the coat to General Grugger. 'I ran it up specially for you, General. You've served me so well, I thought you deserved a little treat.' It was a thin story, but it held off Grugger's suspicions, at least for the moment.

Accepting the coat with a grunt, he tossed it over a chair. 'Are we ready now, then?'

'Well, yes . . .' said the Doctor, unable to think of any more delays.

'So it's just the countdown, and then activation?'

'That's it.'

'All right. Let's do it,' said Grugger.

Brotodac began counting happily. 'Sixty, fifty-nine, fifty-eight . . . '

'No, no, no,' said the Doctor, lying frantically. 'It's not quite as instant as that! The Screens won't reach full activation capacity for about another two minutes. I'm just going to take a stroll outside and try to catch up with myself.'

The Doctor strolled casually to the door. Grugger was peering suspiciously at the settings on the main console which all looked strangely different somehow.

The Doctor paused in the doorway. 'I really don't recommend touching those controls. You might ruin everything.' He went out of the laboratory.

Grugger turned to Brotodac. 'Right, get him!'

'What?' said Brotodac stupidly. 'Get Meglos?'

'Yes. Put him into the spacecraft security hold. We'll keep him alive for a while, just in case, but we can manage without him now – so get him!'

Brotodac hesitated.

Grugger picked up the second coat, the real Doctor's coat from the back of the chair. 'This is yours too, if you want it.'

The second coat tipped the balance. Brotodac turned to the two bemused Gaztaks by the door. 'You heard the General. Get him!'

12

Final Countdown

The Doctor was just walking away from the laboratory when he saw himself—his Meglos self—approaching. Immediately the Doctor ducked out of sight, slipping around the corner of the laboratory and flattening himself against the wall.

The two Gaztaks Brotodac had sent after him didn't see the Doctor, but they did see the approaching Meglos. As they closed in, Meglos stared haughtily at them. 'Shouldn't you two be on patrol?'

One of the Gaztaks punched Meglos very hard in the solar plexus. As he doubled up, they grabbed him by the arms and ran him towards the Gaztak space-ship.

The Doctor winced. 'Very nasty. That could have been me!'

A few seconds later, it was. As the Doctor stepped out of hiding, he ran almost immediately into Brotodac, who had come out of the laboratory to check up on his two guards.

Seeing Meglos apparently still free, and the guards nowhere in sight, Brotodac decided, not for the first time, that if you wanted anything done you had to do it yourself, and hit the Doctor very hard in the solar plexus.

Brotodac caught sight of a patrolling Gaztak and yelled, 'Over here, you, quickly.'

The Gaztak came running over.

Brotodac indicated the doubled-up Doctor. 'Help me get him into the ship!'

They dragged the Doctor away.

Romana, Caris, Deedrix and K9 arrived behind the Screen nearest the Gaztak space-ship, and ducked into hiding. They were just in time to see the two Gaztaks who had grabbed Meglos, leave the ship and resume their patrol.

Minutes later, they saw Brotodac and another Gaztak appear, dragging the Doctor in through the space-ship door.

'I knew he wouldn't get away with it,' said Romana. 'Come on, K9, we've got to get him out.'

'Affirmative, Mistress.'

They crept towards the ship.

Brotodac and the Gaztak dragged the Doctor along a corridor towards the security hold. When they reached it, Brotodac unlocked the door. Without bothering to so much as glance inside, he slung the Doctor in, slammed the door, locked it again, and led the way out of the ship.

Inside the bare metal cell, the Doctor straightened up, rubbing his stomach, and found himself looking at himself. 'Haven't I seen you before somewhere?' he asked politely.

Meglos was too astonished to reply.

Romana and the others ducked round the corner of the space-ship as Brotodac and his Gaztak emerged.

'Stay here,' ordered Brotodac. 'If he tries anything, kill him.' And he hurried away.

Armed, alert and suspicious, the Gaztak stayed on guard.

'We'll never get in the front way,' whispered Caris. 'What do we do now?'

It didn't take Meglos very long to get over his surprise and to realise what had happened. Angrily he paced up and down the little cell. 'Ten thousand years of waiting, planning, and now these Gaztaks have ruined everything. Cretins! Morons! Idiots! Half-wits! Imbeciles!'

The Doctor was lounging back on the hard metal bunk, apparently quite at ease. 'Yes, they've not been terribly clever have they? Not like us!'

'They probably won't even hit Tigella,' raged Meglos.

'If my calculations are correct, they certainly won't!'

'Your calculations?'

'I dropped into your laboratory,' said the Doctor apologetically. 'They thought I was you. I inverted your control settings. If your Gaztak friend starts the countdown, he's going to destroy himself—as well as you and me and the entire planet, of course!'

Grugger stood over the main control console, his fingers drumming impatiently. He looked up as Brotodac entered. 'Well?'

'He's locked away in the security cell. No trouble. Ready now are we?'

'Precisely!' said Grugger, in a very fair imitation of Meglos. 'Prepare for countdown.'

Romana studied the Gaztak guard, who was marching up and down alertly, gazing suspiciously all around. Not an easy man to take by surprise.

She bent down to K9. 'We'll have to use you as a decoy. Off you go!'

K9 trundled slowly into view. Apparently ignoring the guard, he ranged to and fro in a series of semi-circles. The Gaztak looked on in amused surprise, turning slowly to keep K9 in view.

K9 looped round to the other side and the guard turned with him, presenting his back to Romana and the others.

Deedrix crept cautiously forward, and when he was in range tapped the Gaztak on the shoulder. The Gaztak swung round, and Deedrix hit him on the jaw with all his strength. The Gaztak blinked, shook his head, like someone stung by a mosquito, scowled in anger, and raised his blaster. K9 promptly shot him down from the other side. Ruefully Deedrix rubbed his fist. 'Thanks K9.'

Romana and Caris came running forward. 'Quickly,' said Romana, and they dashed into the ship.

They searched the empty ship quickly and efficiently. It didn't take long to find the locked security cell. 'He must be in there,' said Romana. 'Can you open it, K9?'

K9 trundled forwards, protruded his nose-laser, and sent out a searing ray. Slowly a line appeared on the metal door . . .

Meglos was still pacing up and down, up and down. 'Three metres by five metres – and I could have had the galaxy, the universe.'

'You know,' said the Doctor chattily, 'I've often wondered about that.'

'About what?'

'Why should a good-looking chap like you want to control the universe?'

'Why?' screamed Meglos. 'Why?'

'It's always baffled me you know, this burning ambition . . .' the Doctor stopped and sniffed.

Meglos took refuge in his favourite arrogant expression. 'It is beyond your comprehension!'

'Oh, absolutely,' agreed the Doctor. 'Burning . . . ' he said thoughtfully and looked at the door. By now a large section had been almost completely burned away. Suddenly it collapsed inwards, revealing Romana.

'Doctor!' she called joyfully. Then she stopped appalled at the sight of not one but two Doctors. 'Oh good heavens!'

'Out of the way,' snarled Meglos, and tried to push her aside. But Caris and Deedrix were beyond her, blocking his escape.

'Hold him,' shouted the Doctor. 'That's Meglos!'

'You can't take me,' howled Meglos. He was about to hurl himself on the two Tigellans when a faint voice whispered, '*Got you this time, Meglos!*'

119

Meglos went rigid, somehow locked into position where he stood. His skin went cactus green and the tell-tale cactus spines appeared again. The features he had copied from the Doctor began to blur, and another face replaced them. That much-abused Earthling, George Morris, was making another bid for freedom, and he had timed it superbly well.

'*Got you*!' he repeated exultantly, the voice louder, stronger now.

The Meglos voice said, 'On the contrary, Earthling, it's merely you they've got.'

The greenish colour and cactoid characteristics seemed to flow down his body and collect at his feet in a bright green amoeba-like blob. It streaked across the floor and out through the gap cut in the door.

Where Meglos had been was a tall, dark-haired man with a pleasant every-day sort of face, and an expression of total bewilderment and exhaustion. He sank down on the bunk, burying his face in his hands. 'What happened?' he groaned. 'What's going on?'

No one had time to tell him.

'That blob thing – was that Meglos?' asked Romana.

The Doctor nodded. 'What you might call a colourful personality!'

'He must have modulated himself onto a particular wavelength of light,' said Romana, her scientific curiosity aroused. 'With powers like that, Meglos must be virtually indestructible!'

'He may be, but we're not,' said the Doctor briskly. 'We'd better all get back to the TARDIS . . . before it's too late. Your friend Grugger is about to blow up the planet by mistake.'

They headed for the door. The Earthling, however, stayed where he was, on the bunk. Gently the Doctor lifted him to his feet. 'You'd better come too, old chap, unless you'd rather be atomised.'

'Atomised?'

'Yes,' said the Doctor.

'No!' said the Earthling definitely, and followed him from the cell.

Rejoicing in his new-found scientific expertise, General Grugger was busy at the console in Meglos's laboratory. As he worked his mind was filled with dreams of easy conquest. As well as a piece of personal revenge, the destruction of Tigella would be a warning, a demonstration. Once it was complete, he would train the beams on the richest of the nearby planets and send an ultimatum. 'Pay up—everything you have—or go the same way as Tigella.'

It would be almost too easy. Of course, maybe he wouldn't be believed at first and he'd have to blow up a few more planets. Still, that would be no trouble, not now he'd got the hang of it.

Savouring the moment, Grugger said, 'Thirty seconds, beams converging!'

Brotodac began following the countdown on a digital clock that formed part of the main console.

'Twenty-nine, twenty-eight, twenty-seven, twenty-six . . . '

The Doctor bustled his little party into the TARDIS, then, like Romana, paused to give the police box a little pat. 'Now, you're not going to let us down, are you, old girl?'

The TARDIS's take-offs had been a little sluggish lately . . .

In the laboratory, Brotodac went on counting. 'Twenty-five, twenty-four, twenty-three, twenty-two, twenty-one, twenty, nineteen . . . eighteen . . . seventeen . . .'

His voice had all the happy, mindless rhythm of a child playing a skipping game. 'Sixteen . . . fifteen . . . fourteen . . .' A bright green blob shot through the door, across the laboratory floor and flowed into the wilted cactus on its stand . . .

'Thirteen . . . twelve . . . eleven . . . '

The light was flashing on top of the police box, and there was a slow, laborious wheezing groaning sound, but the TARDIS was still obstinately there . . .

Inside, the Doctor and Romana were working frantically at the central console, watched by their astonished passengers.

'You know, Romana,' said the Doctor conversationally, 'it really is time the old girl had a thorough overhaul!'

In the laboratory, unseen by Grugger and Brotodac, the plant had swelled into full fluorescent life on its stand as Meglos resumed his cactoid form.

'Six, five, four . . . ' said Brotodac happily. He wondered if they would hear the bang.

'We're moving!' shouted Grugger in alarm.

'What?' Automatically, Brotodac went on counting. 'Where was I? Five . . . four . . . '

'The laboratory,' screamed Grugger. 'It's sinking again!'

As the laboratory descended beneath the sands of Zolfa-Thura, the TARDIS slowly faded away.

'Sinking?' said Brotodac, puzzled. 'Four . . . three . . . '

Suddenly Meglos's voice boomed through the laboratory. 'Stop the countdown, you fools. The Doctor has tricked you! Stop the countdown!'

Grugger turned and stared stupidly at the plant. 'I can't. The clock's set.'

'Then stop the clock.'

Brotodac leaned helpfully over the console. 'Right you are! It must be this button.'

'Fool,' screamed Meglos. 'Stop him.'

Grugger hurled himself at the console but it was too late. Brotodac's bony finger jabbed a button – the wrong button.

Meglos, Grugger, Brotodac, the Screens, the space-ship, and the whole of Zolfa-Thura vanished in a roaring ball of fire.

The Doctor was standing beside the open door of the TARDIS in the centre of a clearing in a jungle. It was already a very large clearing, and all around gangs of busy Tigellans, Savants and Deons, working together at last, were making it larger still.

This was only one of many clearings in the jungle near the City. The Tigellans were a tough and resilient people and once they had finally accepted that the Dodecahedron was gone forever they had flung their energies into the task of reclaiming the surface of their planet.

Proudly Zastor gestured around them. 'It will be a long hard struggle, Doctor, but at least we have made a beginning.'

Caris and Deedrix paused in their work and came up to them. Caris waved a hand around her. 'We should have done this long ago.'

'I know, I know,' groaned Deedrix. 'You were right all the time. Still, it's better that you were. As Zastor says, it'll be a struggle, but we'll survive.'

'Of course you will,' said the Doctor. 'I'd stay and help, but horticulture isn't really my strong point. Romana's very hot on botany though.' He called inside the TARDIS. 'Romana, what do you know about jungle clearing?'

Romana came out of the TARDIS, followed by the Earthling, Morris. 'A message from Gallifrey, Doctor. They want us back there immediately.'

'Do they indeed?' The Doctor looked grave. Whenever he went back to Gallifrey, home planet of his people, the Time Lords, he always seemed to end up in a great deal of trouble. Still, perhaps this time would be different.

'We'll see about that, after we've dropped our friend here back on Earth.'

He turned to Morris, who was looking considerably better now, though he still had a permanent expression of mild bemusement. The Doctor and Romana had done their best to explain what had happened to him. Very sensibly, Morris had taken the attitude that it was all impossible, but since it had all happened, he had better accept it and forget about it. All Morris wanted now was to get back home and resume his normal life. He swore he would never again complain about the dullness of being an assistant bank manager.

The Doctor turned to him and said, 'Unless of course you want to stay here and do a bit of gardening?'

'Maybe I'd better,' said Morris gloomily. 'I'll be in trouble back home. I told my wife I'd be home in twenty minutes!'

The Doctor grinned. 'Don't worry. All time is relative, you know! Maybe we can get you back before you left.'

'Probably about a hundred years before you left,' thought Romana, but she didn't say it in case she worried Morris. What she did say was 'Come on, Doctor, we really must be going!'

They said their goodbyes to Zastor, Deedrix and Caris, and went into the TARDIS.

Minutes later, a strange wheezing, groaning sound made the toiling Tigellans look up. Quite a few of them saw the TARDIS fade away. Shrugging, the Tigellans got on with their work. A lot of odd things had been happening lately . . .

For once in his lives, the Doctor's spatio/temporal navigation was spot on, and George Morris walked up his garden path just over twenty minutes after he had called his wife. She handed him his glass of medium-dry sherry and kissed him on the cheek. 'Aren't you just a little late today, dear?'

'Am I, darling? Sorry!' said George Morris.

'And you're looking very tired.'

'To tell you the truth, I've been having rather a busy time!'

Mrs Morris knew it was a wife's duty to share her husband's business worries. 'Anything you want to talk about, dear?'

George Morris considered, 'No, I don't think so.' He yawned and stretched. 'What's for supper?'

DOCTOR WHO

	TERRANCE DICKS	
0426114558	**Doctor Who and The Abominable Snowmen**	£1.35
0426200373	**Doctor Who and The Android Invasion**	£1.25
0426201086	**Doctor Who and The Androids of Tara**	£1.25
	IAN MARTER	
0426116313	**Doctor Who and The Ark in Space**	£1.25
	TERRANCE DICKS	
0426201043	**Doctor Who and The Armageddon Factor**	£1.25
0426112954	**Doctor Who and The Auton Invasion**	£1.50
0426116747	**Doctor Who and The Brain of Morbius**	£1.35
0426110250	**Doctor Who and The Carnival of Monsters**	£1.25
	MALCOLM HULKE	
042611471X	**Doctor Who and The Cave Monsters**	£1.35
	TERRANCE DICKS	
0426117034	**Doctor Who and The Claws of Axos**	£1.35
	DAVID FISHER	
042620123X	**Doctor Who and The Creature from the Pit**	£1.25
	DAVID WHITAKER	
0426113160	**Doctor Who and The Crusaders**	£1.25
	BRIAN HAYLES	
0426200616	**Doctor Who and The Curse of Peladon**	£1.50
	GERRY DAVIS	
0426114639	**Doctor Who and The Cybermen**	£1.50
	BARRY LETTS	
0426113322	**Doctor Who and The Daemons**	£1.50

Prices are subject to alteration

STAR Books are obtainable from many booksellers and newsagents. If you have any difficulty please send purchase price plus postage on the scale below to:-

Star Cash Sales
P.O. Box 11
Falmouth
Cornwall
OR
Star Book Service,
G.P.O. Box 29,
Douglas,
Isle of Man,
British Isles.

While every effort is made to keep prices low, it is sometimes necessary to increase prices at short notice. Star Books reserve the right to show new retail prices on covers which may differ from those advertised in the text or elsewhere.

Postage and Packing Rate

UK: 45p for the first book, 20p for the second book and 14p for each additional book ordered to a maximum charge of £1.63. BFPO and EIRE: 45p for the first book, 20p for the second book, 14p per copy for the next 7 books thereafter 8p per book. Overseas: 75p for the first book and 21p per copy for each additional book.